K. J. PARKER

This special signed edition
is limited to 1000 numbered copies.

This is copy **706** .

MIGHTIER THAN THE SWORD

K. J. PARKER

SUBTERRANEAN PRESS 2017

First Edition

ISBN
978-1-59606-817-9

Subterranean Press
PO Box 190106
Burton, MI 48519

subterraneanpress.com

※

Translator's note

Although entirely lacking in literary merit, *Concerning The Monasteries* is a remarkable document in many ways. First and foremost, it is the oldest extant sustained piece of writing in the Robur language, so archaic in places as to be practically unintelligible, but fascinating nonetheless. Second, it was written at the time of the events it records (although see Baines, *AJA* 2007, 42-7 on the serious internal inconsistencies regarding chronology). Finally, it is a personal document rather than a formal chronicle, a unique example from such an early period. It therefore gives us an unparalleled opportunity to hear an authentic voice from the deep past—even if it is not, as Hansen (*CJ* 1987, 33ff) so ingeniously argues, the work of its apparent narrator, nevertheless it is *a* voice, from a world inexpressibly distant and remote from our own.

I have followed Pedretti's Cambridge text throughout, except where specifically noted. I am grateful to Dr John Lancaster of the University of Wisconsin–Madison for his interpretation of the notoriously corrupt final section, and his inspired suggestion of 'linen-press' for *ezaucho*.

※

The usual metaphor is a lighthouse; the monastery as a guttering flame devotedly tended, its small pale gleam resolutely defining the way through the tumultuous storm of barbarism until the Sun rises again—in the East, it goes without saying. They don't have metaphors for the monasteries in the North and the West, where such institutions aren't beautiful images but everyday facts—hard landlords, unreliable business partners, bad neighbours, slow payers. At one time, the cenobitic orders owned two-thirds of the land north of Dens Montis and west of Shevec; they owned the mills and the bridges, the mines, the tanneries, the lumber yards, the forges, the weirs, the moorings, the fishponds, the locks, the ferries, every damn thing you really need. True, they built most of them, nobody else had the money; because the monasteries had taken it all, in rents and tithes. At any rate, that's what they say in the North. I know, because I've been there.

And what do they spend it on, they say in the North, for crying out loud? The usual answer is perfectly true. They spend it on tending the guttering flame; on fifty thousand literate hands, endlessly writing, copying out; on paints and painters, music, sculpture, architecture; on wisdom, beauty, philosophy, mathematics, the glory of the Invincible Sun; on knowledge and truth. A small price to pay, don't you agree, for everything valuable ever achieved by the human race, which only the Orders are left to preserve and maintain in the face of the approaching darkness.

And on other things, too. An insatiable need for vellum and parchment means vast herds and flocks; it also means veal and lamb until you're sick of the sight of it, and you long for a simple bowl of lentil soup.

And other things, too. The monasteries are where the Emperors dump their awkward relatives, out of harm's way, out of sight, out of mind. That or slaughter them; a small price to pay for clemency.

※

EVER SINCE THE Emperor was taken ill, the palace staff have been reporting for their orders to the Empress; five years now, and of course it's only temporary, until His Majesty is up and about again. In practice, this means that when you present yourself at the Lion Gate and bang timidly on the wicket, the kettlehats who peer at you through the little grill are Household Guard, not Companions. I'm all in favour of that. I can see the rationale behind the Companions being recruited exclusively from illiterate barbarians—loyal and answer-able to the emperor alone, therefore outside and above politics, and so forth—but I still think it's nice to have gatekeepers who can understand Imperial. *I have an appointment with the deputy Chief Commissioner for Transpontine Waterways* isn't the easiest thing to get across in sign language.

On this occasion, of course, it wasn't have been a problem. If the Empress sends for you, the herald gives you a dear little ivory spindle, inlaid with emeralds and garnets, which the gatekeeper takes away from you, and then you don't get any bother from anyone.

Some chamberlain in a blue gown with gold tassels relieved me of my helmet and sword and led me up about a million flights of stairs and down a million miles of corridor—I'd just got back from four months on campaign and reckoned I was in fairly good shape, but before long I was sweating and breathing heavily, while this little pot-bellied bald chap trotted happily along in front of me, sandals clip-clopping on the flagstones—until we arrived at the great bronze doors of the Purple, and suddenly I knew where I was. I hung back while he announced me—all the ranks and titles and general scrambled-egg, which I shall never ever learn to associate with my own name—and then I was in; alone in the Presence.

It's all a pose, of course, because everything to do with empire and authority always is, but I have to say, she does it rather well. When the empress grants you an audience, she receives you in the ludicrously-named Small Inner Chamber—it's the size of Permia, but without the rivers—and you stand on one edge of this desert of polished marble while she sits on the other, by the twelve-foot-high window, so as to get the light for her needlework.

It is, let me tell you, the most politicised haberdashery in human history. The pose is; empress of the civilised world she may be, but at heart she's still just an ordinary hard-working housewife, diligent, thrifty, hard-headed, waste-not-want-not. So there she sits, in a gold and ivory chair, wearing a plain dress of worsted she spun herself, turning a shirt-collar or sides-to-middling a bedsheet. She's not just miming, it's genuine work, all the grooms in the Imperial stable wear socks hand-knitted by Her Majesty; and as she sits there, counting her rows and biting off ends of thread, she's doing the budgets of six provinces in her head and calculating a new exchange rate for the hyperpyron against the Vesani thaler.

She didn't look up. "Oh," she said, "it's you."

I mumbled something about reporting as ordered. "Speak up," she snapped. I repeated it, shouting. She thinks it's appropriate for old women to be a bit deaf, though in fact she's got ears like a bat.

"I've been meaning to talk to you," she said, in a voice that made my heart sink. "I saw the reports from Supply. Eighteen thousand pairs of boots in the last six months, and nine hundred tons of chain-mail links. You're seventeen per cent overspent on this year's budget. Do I look like I'm made of money?"

"No, aunt."

"Your father was just the same." She squinted, trying to thread a needle. "I told him till I was blue in the face, it's no earthly use you winning all those glorious victories if you haven't got the money to pay for garrisons and fortifications. You go out there, you kill a hundred thousand savages, then you've got to turn right round and come straight back again. And what does that achieve? Nothing at all, it just makes the savages hate us. Of course he never listened to me, and now look." She thrust the needle and cotton at me. I'm good at threading needles, I've had the practice. "You let the contractors rob you blind, that's what it is," she said. "You just don't think, that's your trouble. You imagine all I have to do is wave a magic wand and suddenly there'll be money. Well, it's not like that."

I cleared my throat. "Actually, aunt, I don't do procurement of supplies, properly speaking I'm not even a soldier any more, I'm an Imperial legate, which means—"

"Oh be quiet." She took back the needle and made a few stitches, neat and infinitesimally small.

"I know what you are, I got you the job, remember, when your uncle wanted to send you to Scaurene. And now I've got another job for you, and let's hope you don't make a complete mess of it."

You could resent a remark like that. Let the record show that over the previous six months I'd negotiated a two-year truce with the Sashan, disposed of the crown prince of Ersevan and hammered out a horrendously fraught alliance with the Blemyans against the threat of the southern nomads. I don't expect any of that to be remembered, because it's all wars that never happened, mighty battles that never got fought, darkest hours of the empire that never had to be faced. But what the hell.

"Of course, aunt," I said. "What can I do for you?"

"It's those wretched pirates." She made the dreaded Land and Sea Raiders sound like a butcher who persisted in overcharging for sausages. "They've attacked Cort Rosch and Cort Seul, burnt to the ground, nothing left. Disgraceful. It's got to stop. So I'm sending you. Pass me the small scissors."

I was too stunned to speak. I passed her the scissors.

ACTUALLY, SHE'S NOT a bad old stick. The strategic mention of Scaurene won't have escaped you; she'll never let me forget that, of course. If you're aware of my dreadful past history, you'll know that I was caught in bed with the Princess Royal, rest her soul, and His Majesty Ultor II, emperor of the known world and brother of the Invincible Sun, was absolutely livid. He wanted to chop my bits off and send me off to a desert monastery, to reflect (his words) on what constitutes acceptable behaviour. But she saved me. She nagged him every morning over breakfast and went on and on at him during his afternoon nap, and just as he was about to fall asleep after a gruelling day's work she'd bring the subject up yet again; *he's only young, give the boy a chance to redeem himself, I owe it to the memory of my poor dear brother, who died saving your life,* over and over again. It's thanks to her I'm writing this, and not frisking my pillow every night for scorpions.

✕

HAVING RECEIVED MY commission, I did what any responsible man does when he's posted to the frontier. I set my affairs in order.

The regular crowd doesn't dig in at the Diligence and Mercy until well after midnight, but I knew she'd be there. I pulled my hood round my face— silly thing to do, it marks you out to everyone in the place as Man Trying Not To Be Noticed, and everybody stares—and asked one of the serving women if she'd seen her.

She looked at me. "Haven't you heard?"

Most of the rest of the night I spent dashing frantically from one miserably depressing charitable institution to another; eventually, just when I'd given up hope, I found her in the Reform House. The bastards, they'd dumped her in the drunk-tank, with nothing but a filthy old blanket and a vague assurance that someone would be along at some point. She lifted her head and frowned at me. "Hello, you," she said.

I nearly broke up. Standing joke between us; her least favourite regular (he's about seven foot tall, absolutely no idea of the concept of personal space) always addresses her thus, and it makes her want to scream. "Hello," I said. "Taking the night off?"

The knife had gone in about an inch to the left of her navel. No way of telling how much blood she'd lost. "I think I might have annoyed him," she said. "How bad is it?"

She knows I know about these things, being a soldier. "It's not wonderful," I told her.

"The bleeding's stopped," she said. Her lips trembled as she spoke. "And it was a clean knife. Mine. You know, the silver-handled one."

She keeps it under her pillow. "We'll have you out of here," I promised her. "I'll get the sawbones from the Twenty-Third, you'll be fine. Just stay there, I'll be right back."

She said something as I ran out, but I didn't catch it. I sprinted up Cartgate, managed to find a

chair—amazing luck—at the Chantry steps; the barracks, I told them, and showed them a five-thaler.
They ran all the way, bless them.

By the time I'd rounded up the doctor (he was
asleep in bed; had to give him a direct order) and
the chairmen had run us all the way back to the
Reform House—I wasn't expecting to find her alive.
I remember praying under my breath all the way, my
life for hers, as though I genuinely believed there was
someone up there to pray to. I don't know. Maybe
there is.

He's a miserable old bugger, that doctor, but once
he sees his patient, nothing else matters. I'd dragged
the chairmen in with me to be porters, and they carried her out like she was made of icing-sugar. "She
can't go back to the barracks," the doctor told me.
"It's against regulations."

I hadn't thought of that; and the doctor's a terror
for the rules. You see, I don't actually have a house,
or a home of any sort; I just camp out in various
palaces. Stupid, really. And that was the first time I
realised it.

I don't have a home but I do have money. "The
Caecilia house on West Hill," I told the chairmen.
"Know it?"

Stupid question; it's one of the principal land-
marks north of the river. They found it just fine;
weren't very happy when I told them to kick the
door down, but another five-thaler changed all that.

"You can't just barge in like that," the doctor said. I glared at him. The house is for sale, I pointed out. I've decided to buy it. First thing in the morning, I'll send someone round to the agents with a draft. Meanwhile, do your fucking job.

I stayed an hour or so, then I couldn't bear it any more; left him to it, told the chairmen (they'd hung around waiting without being asked; amazing how, when the world turns against you, there's so often some too-lowly-to-matter strangers who'll stick by you right to the end) to take me over to the Knights. I woke them up by kicking the door. The man who answered the door was about to call the watch when I told them I was there to buy the Caecilia house.

"It's three in the morning," the man said. "Can't it wait?"

"What's the asking price?"

He screwed his fingers into his eyes and ground the sleep out of them. "Six million," he said.

"Got some paper?"

I wrote out a draft, on the Golden Cross temple, and handed it to him. He stared at it, saw the name; his demeanour changed somewhat. Please come in, he said, sit down, make yourself comfortable. Would you care for some tea and honey-cakes?

Thanks, I said, but I'm in a hurry. He blinked. The keys, he started to say. I told him, that's fine, I don't need any keys.

Funny, isn't it, how there are things—really big, huge, important things that shape and dominate your life—that you don't even know about until something like that happens. I hadn't realised that I had no home. I hadn't realised I loved her, more than anyone or anything in the world.

"It's all right, lads," I told the chairmen, "no need to run."

—Because I was in no hurry to get back to the Caecilia house (now my property, my home). It's better to travel hopefully than to arrive and be told something you don't want to hear. It seemed like it took no time at all to get back to West Hill. Just enough time to prepare my mind, as I've done on a number of occasions in my life. Well, you know what they say. Hope for the best, expect the worst.

So when the doctor scowled at me and said, "She'll be fine," I really wasn't expecting it. That unimaginable surge of relief, that lifts you off your feet.

"Really?" I said.

He gave me a look I deserved. "No, I'm just pretending. Yes, she'll be fine, eventually. Come on, you've seen wounds like that often enough." He frowned, suddenly remembering. "Didn't I stitch you up for something like that?" he said. "The Chloris campaign, about three years ago."

"So you did." I'd forgotten. Shows what sheer terror does to the brain. My guts had been hanging out over my belt. He stuffed them back in, like making sausages. So that was why I'd chosen him for this occasion. Honestly, I'd clean forgotten.

"Well, then. Complete rest and change the dressing twice a day. Can I go home now?"

At that moment I'd have given him anything—the empire, my head, whatever. "Thank you," I said.

"I ought to report this," he muttered at me. "I'm an army surgeon, not your personal bloody physician."

Actually, I think he did. I vaguely remember some talk of a court-martial, which my aunt had to put a stop to. But that was later, and who gives a damn? "Can I see her?"

He shrugged. "I imagine so," he said, "she's ill, not invisible. She's asleep now, don't wake her up. Your chair can take me home."

I gave each of the chairmen a gold tremiss. They stared at me and said how grateful they were. Them grateful to me, for stupid money. Ridiculous.

She woke up just after dawn. By that point, I'd located and hired a fancy society doctor and six nurses; amazing what you can get hold of in the wee small hours if you can pay for it. Something else I'd never realised before, in a desperate emergency, just how useful money can be. I see now why people prize it so highly.

"I've got to go away," I told her, "on business. Won't be too long. When I get back, I think we should get married."

She looked at me. "Are you completely mad?" she said.

"I don't think so. Why?"

Her face was as pale as milk. Inhuman, cross between an angel and a corpse. "One, they won't let you. Two, you don't want to marry me. Three, what on earth makes you think I want to marry you? Or anybody, come to that. Four—"

"You should rest now," I said. "We'll talk about it when I get home."

"Like hell we will. And don't walk away when I'm talking to you."

NOW, THEN. CONCERNING the Land and Sea Raiders. I guess we were so very scared of them because we had no idea who they were, where they came from, how many of them there were, what (beyond anything not nailed to the floor) they wanted. They showed up about a hundred and thirty years ago, during the reign of that old fire-eater Vindex II. Our first experience of them was seventy long, high-castled warships suddenly appearing off Vica Bay. The governor, a civilised man with several well-received volumes of theological essays to his name, sent a message to their leader inviting him to lunch. He came, and brought some friends; it was sixty years before Vica was rebuilt, by which time the harbour had silted up and all the channels had to be dredged out.

Next they manifested themselves as a long column of ox-carts trundling over the Horns. They looked like refugees; skeletal cows and horses, sad women and threadbare children plodding along behind the wagons. The prefect of Garania went out to meet them with relief supplies, food, tents, blankets. They cut his head off and stuck it on their standard, before marching on Beal Epoir and burning it to the ground. That, of course, was about the time when General Maxen was at the height of his incredible career. He caught up with them a week later and hit them so hard that we were sure we'd never hear about them again.

Maxen lasted rather longer than most of our great generals; about six years, and then his head got nailed to the lintel of Traitors' Gate, along with all the others, so that when the Raiders came back there was nobody to deal with them. The next caravan of carts looked like it was here to stay and settle; they hung around for a couple of years, camped beside the ashes of Fort Narisso, dug wells and built sheep-pens and then suddenly disappeared, and where they went to nobody knows to this day. Then fifty years went by and not a sight or sound of them, and people started saying they must've been a myth or an allegory for the plague. And then the ships started appearing right across the northern seaboard, and we gradually came to realise that the ships and the carts were the same people.

Vindex' grandson Florian fought three great battles against them; one by land and two by sea. All three were victories, on a grand scale. After Mount Cortis, they counted the enemy dead by cutting a finger off each corpse, then weighing the filled baskets; half a ton of fingers. It was the Straits of Pallene that led to the growth of the shrimp fishery there, enough food to cause a population explosion. It made no difference at all. Two years later they were back; a hundred ships, a thousand carts. We got the impression that these people, whoever they were, grew like coppice-wood, the more you prune them, the stronger they grow back. Their resources of manpower and materiel were infinite, apparently; ours, of course, were not. It was Ultor's predecessor, Valens IV, who came up with the idea of defence-in-depth; forget trying to turn them back at the border, let them come and do their worst, then hit them on the way back. It didn't work then and it doesn't now, but you're not supposed to say that.

We knew nothing about them then, except that if you hit them just right they died, and we're not much the wiser now. Just goes to show; you can be really intimate with people (what's more intimate than killing?) and still not really know them.

I WAS ISSUED with a commission and letters patent, eight hundred Cassite archers, one million hyper-pyra (in cash, bless her), a pair of fur-lined boots and a letter of introduction to her Serenity the abbess of Cort Doce, who happened to be my aunt's oldest and dearest friend. Thus furnished, I set out to save civilisation as we know it.

It was a bleachingly hot morning, and we were all in our Northern gear, because we wouldn't be needing southern-theatre kit where we were going, so we weren't issued with any. I don't know if you've had much to do with Cassites. They're splendid people, smart, resourceful, imaginative, artistic, individualistic, compassionate, articulate, absolutely useless soldiers. The one thing that marks them out from all the other nations of the empire is their exceptional sensitivity to temperature. In the hall of the prefect's lodgings at Corcina there's a remarkable gadget that tells you what the weather's going to be—there's a dial and a needle that points to wet, windy, sunny, hot, rain, thunderstorm and so forth. Obsolete and redundant, if there's a Cassite in town. You can tell precisely what the weather's going to be just by listening to two Cassites whining. Eight hundred Cassites boiling to death in thick woollen cloaks make a distinctive noise you can hear half a mile away, like roosting rooks or an approaching swarm of locusts.

I was fumbling with my helmet-straps when the message came; looking good, no sign of infection, she's sitting up and demanding to be let out, called you all sorts of rude names. I thanked the messenger and gave him a thaler.

⚹

NOBODY WALKS NORTH if they can help it. The roads are appalling. They used to be wonderful, of course, but that was a long time ago, since when generations of canny farmers have prised up the stone paving-slabs to build pigsties and dug out the rubble and scree for hard standing. Harmodius II tried to do something about it. He decreed the death penalty for anyone found in possession of roadmaking materials. Since enforcing the law would've meant hanging every head of household from here to the coast, nobody was ever prosecuted. If you want to get anywhere, you go by boat.

Four stone-barges carried us down the Sanuse. At Boc Sanis we found wagons waiting for us, which came as a complete and very pleasant surprise. They'd been laid on by the Count of the Northern Shore, a thrice-removed cousin of mine I'd never met by the name of Trabea. He was a big man with a small head, one tiny chin and quite a few large ones, the sort of man you can't help liking and know you shouldn't trust. I'd amused myself on the boat-trip down the river by glancing through his accounts. A child could've seen what he'd been up to, so I took

25

the view that he was confident enough about his position not to give a damn. None of my business anyway, except insofar as I needed to use him.

He filled me in on recent activity over a remarkably fine dinner at the prefecture at Boc. The pirates, he told me, had stepped up their activity over the last eighteen months. During that time they'd stormed three monasteries and seven priories. There had been no survivors. It was hard to tell what they'd stolen, since they'd been to great pains to burn everything.

"What about fittings?" I asked.

He looked at me. "What?"

"Iron fittings," I said. "Hinges, bolts, knockers, nails, all that sort of thing. Stuff that doesn't burn. Did they take them or leave them behind?"

"Oh, I see. No, they left all that."

I nodded. As I told you just now, pirates aren't a new phenomenon. Four centuries ago in the south, there was a wave of similar attacks, only they took everything; they sieved the ashes for roofing-nails. Turned out that what they were after was iron. Hyrcanus III found out where they lived and sent trading-ships, iron for whatever they had a lot of and didn't want—which proved to be ebony, nutmeg, diamonds and lapis lazulae, which is why Hyrcanus is always depicted in portraits wearing a blue cloak. Why strangle a cat when you can drown it in cream?

"How about the people?" I said. "Did they kill them all, or take any?"

He shook his head. "They aren't slavers," he said. "They killed all the monks and nuns and didn't bother the villagers at all. But when we sifted the ashes we didn't find any blobs of melted gold or charred scraps of silk. They're here for the good stuff, I'm sure of it."

All information is useful, even when it confirms what you've already assumed. "There wouldn't be a letter waiting for me, would there?" I asked him.

He looked blank. "No. Should there be?"

Well, no. Civilian mail is carried on the stage, which takes forever to cross the moors. "If something comes for me," I said, "be a pal and send it on, would you?"

He grinned. "Love-letters?"

"I doubt it. Probably the exact opposite."

⌣

THE LIFE CENOBITIC; from time to time it appeals to me, though never for very long.

March into a monastery and pick out ten monks. You'll find you have five religious zealots, two younger sons of good but impoverished families, two political exiles and a retired soldier. Now go next door and round up ten nuns. You'll have six younger daughters of good but impoverished families, three discarded wives and one religious zealot.

I'm talking, of course, about the ones who pray and copy out books. If you extend your sample to the brothers and sisters pastoral—the ones who shear the sheep, make the bread, dig the gardens and wash the bedlinen—you're likely to encounter a fairly homogeneous bunch, farmers and their wives and daughters who've defaulted on monastery mortgages or been sold up for unpaid tithes. It's a viable system, harsh but compassionate; the monastery taketh away and the monastery giveth. Everybody's poor, nobody starves, there's a doctor on hand when they're sick (show me a farmer who can afford a doctor and I'll show you a smuggler or a horse thief) and there's so much veal and lamb that everybody gets some, some of the time. Yes, it's a hard way to treat people. But life is hard, or so they tell me.

✖

MY FIRST CALL was at Cort Malestan. To get there, you go up the coast road until you reach the Red River. It's called that because—well, it's red. The hills above Malestan are full of iron; that's why the monks went there, to dig it out and sell it. The Red River is really quite extraordinary. The water is poisonous. There are no fish, no plants grow in it, a few misguided willows trail their roots in it but they don't live long. It's crystal clear and blood red, if that makes any sense. Local legends say that Hell is under the mountain, and that the monks are there to keep the gates shut with their prayers, but even they can't do anything about the blood of the damned, which seeps out into every rill and stream. The monks have been there for centuries, and they've long since scarfed up all the loose ore lying on the surface or accessible from open pits. These days they drive long galleries into the mountainside. To break up the rock they stuff chambers full of charcoal and burn it till the rock glows red. Then someone opens a sluice on a diverted stream and water floods in; the rock shatters into chunks the size of your fist or your head, which the miners scrabble out into carts. You can see plumes of smoke and steam from miles away, gushing up through dozens of vents. It's not an attractive landscape. But the iron mine is an example of practical alchemy, they turn stone into gold through the application of sweat, and the wealth it produces pays for five hundred copying monks. The Malestan library houses something like eight thousand books, and they send copies of them all over the empire.

In charge of all this is my aunt Thelegund. I say aunt; actually, she's one of my mother's father's nine half-sisters. I chose Malestan as my first call because of her. Before her appointment, she lived at court— that is, before she took rather more interest in politics than was good for her, a classic weakness in our family—and I remembered her from my boyhood as a short, round, jolly old lady who didn't treat me as a child even though I was one. When she got sent to Malestan I wrote her a few letters. It was many years before I found out why she never wrote back—because conducting a secret correspondence with an exiled malignant would've landed me in no end of trouble; try explaining that to a nine-year-old. I was looking forward to seeing her again. So very, very few of my relatives are non-toxic, it'd be a shame to lose contact with one I could actually bear to be in the same room with.

I'd never actually been to a Northern monastery before, so I was expecting something along the lines of what we have back home. I was, therefore, mildly stunned to find that I was approaching, along a wide and beautifully maintained paved road, what appeared to be a castle. It was built on the only bit of flat for miles. Around it was a patchwork of cultivated land—wheat-stubbles at that time of year—out of which it rose like an artificial mountain, as though God had made a toy mountain for his kid to play with, a miniature version of the real thing looming over it on the skyline. Closer up, I admired the quality of the military architecture. Someone had read the right books, and angled the bastions to give enfilading fire from two sides on every conceivable line of approach. The double moat was a nice piece of work. I think it was based on the one at Ap' Escatoy. To fill it, they'd dug a spur off the river, so the moat was blood red and warranted poisonous to all living things; a garish but effective touch. Water for the monastery, I later found out, came from the only sweet-water well in the neighbourhood, which was safely enclosed by the walls.

If you're someone like me, you learn not to take offence easily. Offence, if you're the Empress' nephew, is something that has to be taken seriously and avenged in blood; accordingly, I'm the easiest-going individual you're ever likely to meet. Spit in my face, I'll do everything I possibly can to interpret it as an accident, a joke, a quaint local custom or a back-handed expression of esteem. But being kept waiting annoys me. It's rude. I was, therefore, not in the best of moods after an hour kicking my heels in an ante-room, even though it was one of the most gorgeous and fascinating spaces I've ever been in. For a start, it was floor-to-ceiling with breathtaking frescoes. Heaven forfend that I should ever be mistaken for a man of culture, an aesthete. Those are fighting words at the court of the Emperor Ultor. But even I can recognise the composition, brushwork and light-and-shade effects of the immortal Laiso, the half-blind, cripple-handed divine madman who painted the sort of thing that normally only the gods can see. The whole of the north wall of that ante-room was one huge, heart-stopping Apotheosis. In the bottom left-hand corner cowered Men—pathetic little creatures, ploughmen, foresters, laundrywomen, milkmaids, bare-legged and crumple-faced, shielding their eyes from the radiance of the Invincible Sun as He presents Himself to the world, arms and legs spread wide, head uplifted, the heart of the glowing fire that seemed to fill the whole room—there was no stove or anything in there, but I felt warm just looking at the artwork. Appropriate décor for a room where you wait to see the Sun's temporal representative. But when the Sun's earthly brother is your uncle, with bunches of white hair like asparagus fronds growing out of his ears—well, the effect isn't quite the same.

Well, eventually she condescended to see me, and a monk in a long black robe escorted me up three flights of terrifyingly narrow, slippery-stepped spiral stairs to the Presence.

I don't know what it is about me, but everyone seems to imagine that I'm omniscient. They never tell me anything in advance. They assume I know. Just once, it'd be nice to walk into a difficult situation forearmed. A few terse words would do it—by the way, aunt Thelegund's had a stroke—and then I'd know, and life wouldn't keep hitting me in the face like a carelessly-slammed door.

It didn't help that they'd dressed her up in all the gear. The abbess of Malestan wears the epitrachelion with lorus and zone, the dalmatic, with gold and pearl claves, open at the front with the omophorion draped across the shoulders, the great cope and the two-horned mitre; she holds the globe cruciger in her left hand and the labarum in her right. She was much smaller than I remembered, a tiny little thing, as though someone had put a baby down inside a heap of bejewelled laundry; her head lolled forward, so that the mitre looked like it was going to fall off any minute.

I don't hunt as much as I used to, I don't get the time. But any huntsman would recognise the look I saw in her eyes. You see it in the boar, when its back's been broken and it can't move, or the stag that's been run to exhaustion, or the bird that's been knocked down but isn't quite dead yet. It's the look that says, I'm through, finish me off, please.

The monk leaned close and whispered, "She can't talk but she can hear you." I nodded. If she could hear me, she could hear him, reminding her, though presumably it wasn't something she ever forgot. I cleared my throat. "Hello, aunt," I said. She didn't move.

What the hell are you supposed to say? I never know. The monk stood behind me, respectfully hovering. I had absolutely no evidence to support it, but I got the strongest impression that he was enjoying the sight of her like that. Didn't take much imagination to figure out a hypothesis; she always was a bit hard on servants and subordinates, quite possibly he'd done something to annoy her and she'd had him for it—and then, one morning, like the wrath of God, this. You couldn't resist drawing inferences, could you? You'd take every chance you got to come up here and stand in the doorway where she could see you; possibly a few well-chosen words, when you could be sure there was nobody around to hear. In the circumstances of the contemplative life, I could imagine it was his greatest pleasure and satisfaction.

By one of those coincidences that get to you like a bit of grit in your eye, the sword I was wearing that day was the one she'd sent me for a graduation-day present. If I'd had a shred of humanity I'd have stuck it in her neck as quickly as possible, the way I'd have done without thinking for a buck or a pig. Instead I stood there grinning helplessly for a minute or so, then got out of there as fast as I could, nearly tripped on my cloak going down those horrible stairs.

WHICH BEGGED THE question; if she wasn't running Malestan, who was?

The answer, much to my surprise, turned out to be; nobody. What they'd done was split up the power, like turning a great forest oak into kindling. So long as everything in every department was done exactly the way it had always been done, they reckoned, they could get along just fine—until Her Grace was feeling better, they said, and could resume her duties; or until she died, and some other inconvenient princess was found to take her place.

WELL, I HAD a job to do there. I'm conscientious about my work, though nobody believes it.

I made a thorough inspection of the defences and found them to be admirable—the stonework sound and properly rendered, the woodwork newly tarred, all the chains and lock and hinges in order. I made a point of telling them, if half the cities in the East took as much care over maintenance, things wouldn't be in the state they were in. Then I asked about the garrison. They looked at me. What garrison?

Do you laugh, or cry, or just nod dumbly and change the subject? A magnificently appointed castle, but no defenders. Are there any weapons, I asked. They looked mildly shocked. Naturally, the copying brothers had no use for anything of the kind. What about the lay brothers? Embarrassed pause. No, we don't let them have anything like that. People of that sort, there's no knowing what they might do, especially when they've been drinking. I thanked them and rode away.

⁙

"ALL PERFECTLY TRUE," Count Trabea said. "But there's no reason to suppose the pirates know about it. All they can see is a bloody great big castle. Naturally, they assume the people in it are armed to the teeth."

It goes to show the depths I was sinking to; I'd come to regard Count Trabea as a friend, or at least someone I could talk to, someone who thought the same way and spoke my language. "That's a big assumption," I said. "Bearing in mind we know nothing at all about these pirates."

He shrugged. "They've left Malestan alone, haven't they? One thing I'm fairly sure of, they don't have any sources of local information. All they know is what they can see. And what they can see is a double moat and huge, newly-mended walls. I don't think you need worry unduly about Malestan."

"You're probably right," I said. "Oh, by the way, any letters come for me while I was away?"

He shook his head.

✕

THE MONKS HAD given me a present, to thank me for advising them. It was about the size of a paving-stone, wrapped in a red silk cloth; no prizes for guessing, a book. Now I'm not a great reader, but a Malestan folio is a gift fit for a king. I waited till I was alone in my tent, and unwrapped it.

The cover was the sort of rich dark brown leather they make the very finest boots from; split calf, if I'm not mistaken, oak-tanned with eggs rather than brains, skived into three and worked for a whole day on the stretchers to get it beautifully supple. It was embossed with a falconry scene; four men and a fine lady in a wimple have launched a goshawk, which

takes a heron in mid-air; below, the dogs peer hopefully upwards, in case they're needed to retrieve.
I opened it. The title page was stunningly illumi-
nated in gold, red, blue and green interlocking swirls
and clusters, each colour bordered in black. Follow
one line, then switch to another and the perspec-
tive shifts vertiginously, making your head swim;
blue dives under red and over gold, branches out
to enfilade and encircle green, explodes into a delta
of tendrils, interlaced but never tangled, each one
a clear narrative—but where each colour ends and
where it begins is impossible to determine, until
eventually it dawns on you that each thread isn't a
line but a loop, perpetually circulating, like blood
or the circuit of the stars. In the centre of all this
was a miniature of the Invincible Sun *orans*, palms
uplifted and facing, His head encircled in a glowing
gold halo, his eyes dark, compassionate, disturbing;
at the corner of the left eye, a single unexplained
teardrop. I went to turn the page, but I didn't want
to break the eye contact; I sat quite still, looking at
Him as He looked into me, until my heart was perfectly empty. Then I closed the book and wrapped
it up in its sheet.

I forget what the book was; the *Sermons of
Perceptuus* or something like that.

✤

CORT DOCE WAS next. I handed over my letter of introduction.

I could see why Abbess Svangerd and my aunt had always got on so well; also why they'd chosen to live so far apart. Two somewhat forthright women who value a friendship too much to risk damaging it by close proximity; don't have two flints rattling around in a small box if you don't want sparks.

You could tell Svangerd had been a raging beauty once, just as she wasn't one now. Old age had parched her, where it had swollen my aunt; she had bones you could've shaved with. Even now she was tall, probably an inch taller than me and I'm six foot; I couldn't judge properly because she stayed sitting all the time I was with her. She wore a plain black gown with a single thin line of silver thread at the neck and cuffs; somehow she made it look almost wickedly elegant. She nodded at me to sit down on a rickety little stool with three spindly legs. It took my weight with a few creaks of protest. Then she read the letter.

Svangerd and my aunt were from the same village, somewhere up in the north-eastern mountains—I don't know where, and nobody wants to find out. They both lost their families to the plague when they were kids; nothing left for them in the village, so they walked down the mountain to the nearest city, looking for work. Is that the right word? I guess it is; work is what you do to make a living. If your work happens to be someone else's pleasure, it's still work, isn't it? Anyway, they both turned out to be extremely good at it. Word quickly spread, and they graduated from the provinces to the big city, from a high-class cathouse in the Goosefair to their own exclusive establishment on Temple Hill. Reliable accounts of that era in their lives are hard to come by, since nearly all their regular clients either died or received a sudden, urgent vocation to the monastic life, not long after my aunt married general Ultor, as he then was. When Ultor was called to the Purple, Svangerd announced that she was quitting the business and wanted a monastery, preferably a big, rich one, a long way from Town. It was a graceful thing to do (and it's always better to volunteer than be dragged away by the hair), and they've maintained their friendship ever since.

She lifted her head and looked at me. "She says you're here about the pirates," she said, as though I was the man come to fix the weathervane. "Well? Have you got a strategy?"

"Not yet," I said. "I don't know enough about the situation."

A good answer, apparently. She nodded. "I can help you," she said. She picked up a brass tube and handed it to me. "That's everything I've been able to find out about them," she said. "It's not very much, but it'll give you somewhere to start. Kremild says you're quite bright."

Stunned isn't the word. "Does she?"

A faint smile. "Reading between the lines," she said. "But you know what she wrote, surely." I looked blank. She frowned. "You read the letter, didn't you?"

"No," I said. "It was sealed. And anyway, I don't—"

"My God." She raised both eyebrows. "Before you leave," she said, "I'll teach you how to lift a seal so that nobody will ever know." She looked at me for a moment, as though I was something brought back by travellers from a distant land. "A word of advice, if I may presume. If a superior gives you a letter to be delivered unopened, *always* open it. One time in a hundred it'll say something like *the bearer of this letter is to be put to death immediately.*" She picked up a little brass bottle, showed it to me and put it away in the handsome walrus-ivory box on the table. "Won't be needing that now," she said. "So is that all you are? A good soldier?"

"I'm not a soldier," I said. That fleeting glance of a small brass bottle—it was like when you inadvertently look straight at the sun, and when you look away, there's a big raw red patch in the middle of your vision. "I'm an Imperial legate."

She grinned at me. "I knew your father," she said. "He was much younger than Kremild and me, of course. When the plague killed his parents, the neighbours took him in. A boy, you see, he'd be useful on the farm. We sent for him as soon as we could, and Kremild got him a commission in the Guards.

You're a lot like him. Solid. I expect you'll be the next emperor."

I stared at her. "I sincerely hope not," I said.

She laughed. "I believe you," she said. "Now, I've given orders for your men to be quartered on the lay brethren. They won't like that, but they'll just have to put up with it. You can use the library, obviously. I have good couriers, they can be in Town in three days. Naturally, you'll use this as your headquarters."

"Actually—"

"Splendid. Don't trust Count Trabea any further than you can kick him. I don't know what enemies you may have at home, but he'll definitely be out to get you. Poison, almost certainly, but not in your food, he's smarter than that. If you get a cut or a scratch, don't have a local doctor see to it. And don't sleep in a tent with a charcoal stove. It's amazing the number of people who've asphyxiated in their sleep since Trabea took office."

I was feeling a bit dizzy. "Why would Trabea—?"

"Because he hasn't been doing his job properly, or you wouldn't be here. And it's not a difficult job, and Trabea's a very competent man, so you have to ask yourself, why has he failed?" She smiled at me. "I'm forgetting my manners," she said. "Would you like something to drink?"

"No thank you."

She laughed again; silvery, like a young girl. "It's all right," she said, "you can trust me, Kremild's told me to look after you. It's everybody else you should be terrified of. Have some wine, it'll put colour in your cheeks. We make a passable white, even this far north. It's quite dry but with a rather pleasant flowery aftertaste."

"Convenient."

"Oh, don't be silly." She gave me a stern look. "Now, then. Getting rid of these wretched pirates is important," she said, "so I'll expect you to put some effort into it. Clearly Kremild thinks so too, or she wouldn't have sent you." She studied me for a moment, the way I've seen butchers look at carcases. "I imagine you think the monasteries are just irrelevant monks and inconvenient royal women. You're wrong. Actually, they're the only justification I've ever managed to come up with for the empire. Did your aunt ever tell you how the plague came to our village? There was an outbreak among some auxiliary cavalry just arrived from Sembrotia. As soon as the symptoms were confirmed, the governor had them driven out of the city, with no food or water. They went looking for something to eat; they found us. We didn't know about plague, of course, what the symptoms are or anything like that. We took them in and tried to look after them." She shrugged. "It wasn't anybody's fault. But it takes an empire to hire nomads in Sembrotia and bring them all the way to the Western mountains. That's what empires do, they bring people together, make connections." She opened the ivory box and put away a small penknife and a stick of sealing wax. "They make it possible to build great libraries, places like this, that endure. The same plague that killed my village wiped out all the monks at Cort Valence. They all died, but the books remained intact. One of the first things I did when I came to this house was send two dozen carts and have them brought here, where they're safe. In the end, you see, books are all that matter. How did Saloninus put it, the past speaking to the future? It's what survives, you see. When those carts arrived from Valence, I found all three books of Licinius' *Eternal Crown*. The third book's been lost for centuries, and it's the only record of the Seventh Dynasty. Just a few sheets of parchment, that's all, but in it is all that's left of four hundred years of people's lives. And there was Pacatian's *Mechanics*, and four completely unknown dialogues of Constans. That's what we are here, we're beachcombers finding little scraps and fragments of wrecks on the beach. It's only scraps, but it's *everything*." She shrugged. "And the pirates will just burn it all, if we let them. Do you understand what I'm saying?"

"I think so," I said awkwardly. "And yes, obviously—"

"This is no good." She stood up, a little stiffly. "I'll have to show you. Follow me."

I'll say this for her, she was quicker up and down those stairs than I was. We went all the way down, then across a courtyard and a stable yard, through a doorway and down a very long stair until we reached a big oak door. She took a lantern down off the wall. On the other side of the room there was nothing; just an empty cellar, that's all.

"Over here," she said.

She held up the lantern, and I looked into its pool of light. "It's a wall," I said.

"There's half a million people in this room. Look closely."

I looked, and I believe I could just make out some marks on the wall. "What's that?"

"Writing," she said. "Very old writing."

"Ah. What does it say?"

"I have no idea." She'd been holding the lantern at arm's length; tiring. She lowered it, and its light was confined to a square yard of floor. "That's the point. That bit of wall is all that's left of the building that was here before we came. We don't know how old it is, or who built it, or what the writing says. That's the point. Calyx's *Chronicles* give us the history of this region for the past thousand years, but he doesn't say anything about anybody living here. Whoever *they* were, they've gone for ever, as though they'd never existed. That's all that's left of them, those letters on a stone slab, and we can't read them." She raised the lantern again. "Do you understand now?"

I nodded. I don't like dark rooms underground, and I wanted to get out of there. "Yes," I said.

Actually, I'd have agreed with anything for a chance to get back into the open air. Half a million people in one room; she'd made her point. From where I was standing—maybe it's a morbid dread of ending up in a cell for the rest of my life, *cell* being an ambiguous term; such a fear being understandable, given our family history—it felt more like half a million prisoners, yearning to be free.

※

YOU'RE SAFE IN a prison. They bring you your food, regular as clockwork. Most cells are a bit damp, but nothing compared to the sort of houses most people in the north-west have to live in. And there are armed guards on every door, so your chances of being cut down by hordes of vicious marauders are practically nil.

I remember visiting my father in one of those places. The poor fool said he was happy. He lay on his back, arms behind his head; this is the life, he said. I can lie around all day, read when I feel like it, do a bit of exercise, and I don't have to do any work—work being ruling and governing, issuing orders, deciding destinies, signing death warrants. And no visitors (he grinned at me when he said it); no visitors is absolute fucking bliss, after all those years with my family. Finally, he said, after a lifetime in the conflict business, I can get some peace.

The ambiguity of the word *cell*; keep an eye on it.

✕

BEFORE I SET off for Sambic, she sent for me. There was a letter on her desk. One of my most useful survival skills is the ability to read upside-down. The letter was from my aunt; I recognised the handwriting before Svangerd could cover it up.

"She's worried about you," she said.

"Really?" The surprise was genuine. My aunt's always given me the impression that she believes me to be immortal, invulnerable and immune to all known diseases; or else why would she keep sending me to the wars?

"She thinks you're on the verge of making a most unsuitable marriage."

Oh. "She turned me down," I said.

"I know." Svangerd looked at me, just briefly. "She's fine, by the way. Not your aunt. Whatsername. What in God's name possessed you to spend six million on a house for a prostitute who refuses to marry you?"

I grinned feebly. "It was the middle of the night."

When you're as smart as Svangerd, I guess you get out of practice hearing things you can't understand. She scowled. "What?"

"She was very badly injured and I needed to find some place where the doctor could treat her. I don't have a house of my own, and I couldn't think of anywhere. Then I remembered the Caecilia house was for sale, which meant it'd be furnished but empty. She needed to be treated straight away. So I told them to take her there. We kicked the door down to get in."

She sighed. "Yes, all right," she said. "But *buying* the place—"

I shrugged. "It was simpler that way."

She gazed at me for an uncomfortably long time, as though she was doing complicated mental arithmetic. "Your aunt thinks you should have nothing more to do with this female," she said. "I'm not sure I agree."

I didn't know what to say, so I made a sort of grunting noise. Bad habit of mine.

"Your aunt," she went on, "maintains that if you marry a tart, it'll look like a declaration of intent to try for the throne."

I opened my mouth and closed it again.

"Think about it. Ultor married your aunt, and three years later he was crowned. By following in his footsteps, so to speak, you're making a loud, clear statement. You're saying, I don't give a damn what people think, because quite soon I'll be emperor and I'll do what I like. Your aunt believes you don't yet have enough of a power base for that sort of gesture. I have to say, I beg to differ. I think that by biding your time, keeping out of the cut and thrust of politics and doing dull but worthy things out on the frontiers, you've lined yourself up as the obvious compromise candidate, for when the Optimates and the Populists tear each other to pieces. Also, marrying this woman will be seen as you deliberately putting yourself out of the running for the throne; so, of course, people will say, here's a man who isn't hell-bent on the Purple, if we make him emperor he'll be sensible and moderate, because that's how their minds work." She nodded. "Svangerd won't listen to a word I say, naturally, we've known each other far too long. But my advice is, go ahead. It's a gamble, but what isn't?"

"I love her," I said.

For a long time she didn't say anything, just considered me, in the abstract. "Have a safe trip," she said.

✕

WHILE I WAS on the road from Cort Doce to Cort Sambic, the pirates attacked. They appeared out of nowhere—our lookout station on the headland at Petrobol saw nothing—and burned Cort Amic to the ground. By the time I got there, all that was left was ash.

There's a large, quite prosperous village at the foot of Amic Hill. The monks had a sawmill there, and a tannery, and a substantial clay pit, with a brickworks and a pottery. The first thing they knew about any attack was a bright light on the hilltop, sunrise in the middle of the night. Being sensible people, they ran into the woods and didn't come out until their scouts promised them it was safe; about an hour before I turned up. No help from them, then.

I set my Cassites to picking through the ashes for bones. Skulls, I told them, were the thing to look for, since a human being has only one head, and I needed to know if the entire complement was accounted for. I came up short; there were a hundred and sixteen praying monks, ninety-seven nuns and a hundred and forty-two lay brethren, but all we could find was two hundred and seventy-six skulls. I could live with the discrepancy. A good hot fire, such as you get from burning dry wood or dry paper, will consume bone completely. It all depended on where in the building they were. Of the two-hundred-seventy, fifty-three skulls showed evidence of crushing, cutting or piercing. We also recovered forty-seven arm and leg bones that showed blade-marks. Inconclusive; but the impression I got was of monks and nuns cut down in a general fox-in-the-henhouse panic, rather than the more systematic approach I'd been postulating—the entire congregation herded into the temple or the chapter-house, say, and then burnt alive. I didn't get a chance to make the sort of detailed analysis I'd been hoping for, because it came on to rain and turned the ash to black mud. But we sifted trial areas with sieves, and came up with bone and metal fragments and charred timbers we could identify as heavy furniture. The metal was almost all iron. There was something about the ash I couldn't quite understand, but as I said, the rain came and put a stop to my speculations.

✕

I WAS TEMPTED to head back to Cort Doce and cor-
relate what I'd found with the report Svangerd had
compiled for me, but my schedule said Cort Sambic
was next, so that was where we went. Needless to
say, when we got there we found them in a pretty
desperate state. Sambic was even better fortified than
Cort Doce, and when we got there, all the monks
were on the wall, praying brethren as well as lay; as
soon as we came in sight they started making the
most appalling racket, banging on tin buckets and
saucepan-lids, as though we were rooks on the spring
wheat. They didn't want to open the gate, even when
I walked up alone and bare-headed, with my warrant in my hand. They didn't believe me. I could've
waylaid a genuine Imperial legate, cut his throat and
stolen his credentials. I think they'd have shot arrows
at me if I'd hung about any longer. So we pitched our
tents in the Foregate, and I sent a rider back to Doce;
could Svangerd please spare a couple of irreproach-
ably genuine monks to vouch for me? They came the
next day—amazingly fast—in a beautiful low-sprung
chaise drawn by four thoroughbred Hill Aelians (you
wouldn't find better horses in the Hippodrome back
home), and after a rather embarrassing yelling-at-
the-tops-of-our-voices conference under the guard
tower, we were acknowledged as authentic government agents and allowed in through the door.

The abbot of Cort Sambic was a complete surprise.

"Stachel?" I didn't mean to shout. "What're you doing here? Aren't you dead?"

He gave me a stone-face, dignified look. "It's a grey area," he said. "Come in and have a beer."

Once I'd seen Stachel, Sambic made sense. It wasn't just a fortress, it was *the perfect* fortress, as described by Vitalian in the *Mirror of Warlike Virtues*. Very recently, within the last ten years, someone had miraculously found the money and the labour and the time and the energy to follow Vitalian's blueprint down to the letter—triple walls, staggered gateways, huge fat dirt bastions to soak up artillery bombardments, projecting galleries to frustrate scaling ladders, the whole nine yards, with some wild-eyed enthusiast directing the work with his thumb stuck between the pages of the book to mark the place. Guess who gave Stachel a copy of Vitalian, as a birthday present, because he couldn't afford to buy one for himself?

"It's a grey area," he said, snapping his fingers to summon attendants, "because when a man joins the holy monks, he's deemed to undergo death of the earthly body and rebirth as a new spiritual entity, which is why he takes a new name and has nothing more to do with his disreputable friends from the old days. No, don't sit on that one, it's pretty but it won't take your weight."

I sat on a stool. "You're dead," I repeated. "They cut off your head, for crying out loud. I went and saw it on the Northgate."

He shrugged. "You're confusing me with someone else," he said. "Mind you, I seem to remember there was this cooper's apprentice in Lonazep who looked a bit like me, or would've done if someone had smashed his face in with a hammer and pulled out all his teeth. Maybe it was his head you saw. I wouldn't be a bit surprised if he came to a bad end. Anyway," he added, with a huge grin, "how the devil are you? What's she like?"

So that was how they'd managed it. I'd wondered, at the time. His parents had been so cool and stoical; our son has been found guilty of conspiring against the Emperor, we're not sorry he's been executed, we're glad the plot was detected in time. Still, a monastery. I'd have thought Stachel would've preferred the axe. Though I don't imagine they gave him the choice.

"What's who like?"

"This girl," he said. "The tart you bought a six-million-tremiss house for. What can she do that's worth that sort of money?"

When I knew him Stachel couldn't afford his own copy of Vitalian, but he had quite a few books, the sort with pictures in. He'd always been of an academic turn of mind. He used to talk about collating all the available source material, adding in the results of his own extensive researches and compiling the definitive work on the subject—sort of an equivalent to Vitalian's *Mirror*, but with full-page coloured illustrations. I wouldn't last five minutes inside his head.

"I have no idea what you're talking about," I said. "Are you really an abbot? I can't believe it."

Two tall men in elegant grey gowns brought us honey-cakes and sweet fortified wine in tiny silver beakers. "Screw you, then," he said, knocking his wine back in one. I knew better than to try. "I started off as a simple novice, no name, no past or antecedents. I got this far by sheer unadulterated merit, because I happen to be an outstanding scholar. And a damned good administrator, come to that."

I tried one of the biscuits. Excellent. "You're very young to be wearing the silly hat," I said.

He nodded. "Second youngest in history, discounting the political appointments," he said. "If you gave a stuff about spiritual matters you'd have come across my five-volume commentaries on Sechimer and my proposed revision of the minor catechism. As it is—"

A light glowed in my head. "Oh, you're *the* Honestus," I said. "Sorry, I didn't make the connection. Anyway, I'd assumed he was someone a hundred years ago."

He looked up. "So you've read them?"

I pulled a face. "The commentaries, sorry, no," I said. "The catechism, yes, of course."

"What do you think?"

There was an eagerness in his voice I remembered so well; drunken adolescent discussions of the Nature of the Soul in noisy bars, surrounded by bad company. "I'm not sure," I said.

"Oh."

"You put your case too well. Any argument so elegantly and persuasively presented makes me suspicious."

He hated me for a second and a half, then shrugged. "I let myself get carried away," he said. "It's like decorating a chapel. Why just have carvings and mosaics when you can have frescoes and gilded mouldings as well? And the result's not the splendour of God, it's bad taste."

Later, when I'd retired to bed with a slightly thick head, I reflected on Stachel and me. When he was arrested, I did everything I possibly could, used all my connections and influence; deaf ears, coupled with grim warnings about choosing my friends more carefully. I couldn't understand why I couldn't save him, being who I was, until it dawned on me that I was nobody special, after all; that there were ever so many things the Empress' nephew couldn't do, and the only result of trying was getting myself in trouble. That realisation had a big effect on me, and I vowed to learn the lesson; humility, realism, think about what you're doing, how it'll impact on you and other people. But of course it wasn't like that. Execute the Empress' nephew's best friend? Of course not. Instead, we cut off the head of some poor innocent apprentice and crush it in a mortar till it can be mistaken for him, and then we send the friend to a distant monastery and make sure he does well (though Stachel didn't seem to have guessed that bit; he's bright, but he has a high opinion of himself). And they didn't tell me at the time because I'm a known blabbermouth, and afterwards it must have slipped their minds, the way things do. It's a bit like finding out, late in life, that the Invincible Sun made the sky blue because He knew it's your favourite colour.

I also considered the fact that Stachel got in all that trouble because he was part of a conspiracy to murder my uncle and aunt, and quite possibly me as well, for tidiness' sake, and at the time that thought never entered my head. Was he still a red-hot republican? You think you know people.

Actually, I remember the cooper's boy. He was no good anyhow and no great loss. Even so.

※

"Trabea is an arsehole," Stachel told me, as I got ready to leave after a much longer stay than I'd anticipated. "You really want to watch him. He's corrupt and greedy and lazy and treacherous, and as soon as you get home you want to get him recalled and strung up."

I nodded. "You don't like him much."

Stachel frowned. "Actually I do," he said. "He can be very charming, and occasionally very thoughtful, and efficient, so long as what you want fits in with one of his personal agendas. And he makes me laugh, which is a special blessing. But a lot of bad people are very likeable, and a lot of good people are boring and dead miserable."

"I'll watch out for him," I said.

Stachel nodded, satisfied that I'd taken the point. "They say he's got a Scherian doctor who knows every single poisonous substance in the world," he said. "Snake venoms, mushrooms, berries, seeds, special kinds of mould you sprinkle on cheese, the lot. If you get sick, for pity's sake don't let him near you."

He poured himself a drink, offered me one, which I refused. "What can you tell me about Cort Auzon?"

He shook his head. "No more than you'll have read already in your briefing notes. It used to be a great house with a fantastic library, but it fell on hard times about fifty years ago, nobody knows why, and now they haven't got two coppers to rub together." He scratched his ear. "I sent a man over there, year before last, offered to help them out by buying some of their books. He came back with a shipload, literally—one of those barges they use for hauling bulk timber, and it was riding dangerously low in the water. Complete mixture of junk and treasure, they must have just pulled books off the shelves at random. That's how the fifth eclogue of Ausonius came to light, when we all thought it had been lost five hundred years ago, and three brand new Terpaio comedies." He smiled. "Don't worry, I've got my boys copying them for you right now, soon as they're done I'll send them on. The abbot's a man called Gensomer, but I don't know a thing about him."

✶

HALFWAY FROM SAMBIC to Auzon—by land—is the *Hope of Redemption*, a big old inn that used to be an Imperial staging post, when we still ran a regular mail beyond the mountains. I expected it to be quiet—actually I expected it to be derelict, with no roof and thistles growing up through the kitchen floor—but in the event I had to wave my warrant around before I got a room, and that meant turning out a prosperous merchant, his wife, son and three daughters. The Cassites pitched their tents in some poor devil's hay meadow (we're not suppose to pay compensation because of setting precedents, but I do) and I sent a military tribune, in full armour and regimentals, to terrify the kitchen staff into heating me some water for a bath.

"You're busy," I said to the landlord.

"No more so than usual."

I asked him about that. Apparently, over the last few years, a brisk trade had started up between our north coast and the Fleyja Islands, which are silly little bits of rock out in the deep, stormy sea. I didn't know anybody lived there, but apparently they do, and they have amber, beaver pelts for making felt for hats, freshwater pearls, hops and huge quantities of small, smooth-shelled walnuts, no good for eating but just right for making oil. In return we trade them wheat, wool, salt and copper. Amazing, the things that go on that we don't know about. Apparently it's worth it for some of the great merchant companies from the City to send stuff up here, in spite of the cost and the risk. You'd have thought some of them might have seen fit to mention all this to the government, but I can see why they haven't; we'd start levying taxes, and maybe send a fleet to conquer the islands, and once government barges in, the days of easy profits and quick returns are over and done with. I gather the Fleyja people use their own boats, which are stupid little things, no more than faggots of twigs tied together with rope and decked over. Hundreds of them drown every year, but that doesn't stop them coming.

The bath was an enormous terracotta thing, like the clay coffins of Blemya, where they bury their dead sitting up. The water was warm, and there was a china sprinkler for sand and a Mezentine jar of rose-scented oil, and a bronze scraper in the shape of a leaping dolphin.

I'd just got out, and was drying myself off in a sort of warm, cosy daze, when one of my tribunes banged on the door. "You'd better see this," he shouted. He sounded rattled, and it takes a lot to do that to a Guards officer.

I threw on my tunic and cloak and stumbled out onto the balcony. Below in the courtyard, I saw something that turned my knees to water; an Imperial courier's chaise, with six heavy lancers for an escort.

They haven't built one of those chaises for fifty years, but no need, they made them to last. They look so frail and delicate, you can't believe they'd stand up to five minutes over the ruts and potholes, but they go like the wind, drawn by four of the best horses you'll ever see anywhere. I've ridden in one about a dozen times, and the springs are so good you can put a glass of wine down on the floor and it won't spill a drop. Even so; an Imperial courier is the last thing a general on campaign wants to see, because it's a surer bet than the Emperor's horse in the Hippodrome that out of it will climb an Imperial legate, bringing you a summons, in purple ink with the Dragon seal; return to the City immediately to answer charges. I was there when the chaise came for my father—don't worry, son, he told me, this is just some stupid misunderstanding, I'll be back again before you know it. I wanted to go with him but he wouldn't let me.

I remember thinking a lot of things, between the driver jumping down and unfolding the steps and the door opening. One of them was, *it's not fair, I haven't done anything*, which shows how naïve I was, even then. Also selective with my memories. Everyone who's carried the Imperial warrant's done something, at one time or another, and I'm definitely no exception. And I remember thinking, *it's all right, aunt won't let anything happen to me*, followed by *what if it's her who sent the coach?* And then the door opened, and the last person in the world I expected to see got out.

I leaned over the balcony and shouted; "What the hell are you doing here? And what do you mean by giving me the fright of my life?"

She was terribly pale, and she was leaning on a stick. "Pleased to see you too. Didn't you get my letter?"

Nothing, especially the mail, travels as fast as the couriers; but maybe she didn't know that. "What are you doing here?" I repeated; and then, "How are you?"

"Still alive," she said. "Now find me somewhere I can lie down, before I fall over."

⸎

You've got to hand it to her. "I made your man Mnesarchus break into your desk and steal your signet ring," she told me calmly. "And then I made him forge me a travel warrant, and then we went to the courier's office and they gave me this coach. And the six bull-eaters, which I confess I wasn't expecting. Still, they look pretty in their shiny trousers."

As simple as that. I made a vow to send Mnesarchus to the slate quarries, and a moment later another one to bring him back and give him a nice farm somewhere. "I'm going to be in so much trouble," I said.

She grinned. "Really."

"You bet. Misuse of the Imperial courier, forgery of the Imperial seal—"

"It was your ring."

"Yes, but I'm not supposed to have it, am I? And I'm most definitely not supposed to use it to transport my tart du jour halfway across the Empire. My aunt is going to skin me alive."

She thought about that. "I doubt it," she said. "It shows style, and a total disregard for the rules and conventional opinion. People like that sort of thing in an emperor. He broke the rules to be with the woman he loves."

"I'm not the emperor. I will never be the emperor. That pinhead Scaurus is going to be the next emperor." I stopped and gave her the nastiest look I could summon up. It made her giggle. "Is that why—?"

"Don't be stupid," she said, and I believed her. "But your aunt won't be cross, though she'll probably write you a rude letter. She wants you to start acting the part."

I was suddenly furious. "How the hell can you say that? You don't know her, you've never met her."

She sighed. I could see how tired she was. "You talk about her enough. I probably know her better than most people. Definitely better than you do. And she'll be fine about it. She's got much more important things to worry about, believe me."

I was still trying to be angry, but it was getting harder and harder. "I asked you a question," I said. "Why are you here? You must be mad, thirty hours in a coach with your belly full of needlework."

She smiled at me. I love her so much. "It was you asked me a question," she said. "Well, you made it into an order, but you know I never do what you tell me to."

I couldn't speak. She waited, then went on, "Well, I thought about it a lot, and I decided that probably this—" she pointed "—was a hint that I ought to retire, and that begs the question, what do I do now? And most of us in the trade try and sucker some poor fool into marriage. And I thought, I know a poor fool who'll do. So here I am."

"Yes?"

"Yes."

Strange how you react sometimes. Several times I'd tried to imagine the moment when she said she'd marry me, and always, in my imagination, I whooped with joy and ran through the streets yelling at the top of my voice. Wasn't like that. I just stood there, still as a rock, while the completely changed and utterly transformed glorious new world enveloped me. "Good," I said. "And now my aunt really is going to kill me."

She changed instantly to a serious face. "I don't think so," she said. "You're following precedent, the best possible precedent in the world, from her point of view. Of course, you're going to have to change your name."

Turned over two—no, make that three—pages at once. "You what?"

"To Ultor. Then you'll be Ultor the Third. Continuity," she said. "At the moment, it's what the empire needs more than anything else. But no, your aunt will be fine. You don't seriously believe I'd be here if I didn't think so."

"Yes, but—"

"This is something you need to do. Politically," she added quickly. "Politics is all gestures, and you don't have a clue when it comes to gestures. But this is a good one, which is why I've agreed. Politically—"

"Will you shut the fuck up about politics," I said, and kissed her.

A moment later she yelped with pain and I let go. "What did the doctor say?" I asked.

She hesitated, just a little. "No permanent damage," she said. "An inch to the left, I'd have been dead. I think they always say that."

I've heard it myself a few times. "You shouldn't have come," I said. "What if you'd burst the stitches? It was a ridiculous risk to take."

She gave me her you're-impossible look. "It was a gesture, stupid," she said. Then that serious look again. "Are you happy?"

"Yes," I said. "For the first time in my life, there'll be someone I know is on my side. You have no idea what that means."

She nodded gravely. "No matter what," she said. "And don't worry about your aunt. When she looks at me, it'll be like looking in a mirror. And no woman can resist doing that."

I HAD TO send the chaise back, but we had a stroke of luck. One of the merchants at the inn agreed to sell us his luxury coach—for a ludicrous sum of money, and only after I'd threatened to requisition it. It wasn't as sleekly efficient as the government chaise, but speed was no longer of the essence, and it was damnably comfortable.

"I won't be able to go in it, naturally," I said mournfully.

"No?"

"Of course not. I've got to ride at the head of the damn column, it's expected of me."

"Poor baby." She pulled a wonderfully soft-looking rug over her knees and plumped up the cushions.

"And will you have to eat barley porridge and drink horse-piss, just like the men?"

"Not the horse-piss. That's only in the desert."

She raised her eyebrows. "They packed me a hamper at the inn," she said. "There's smoked lamb sausage with truffles."

"I don't love you any more."

She smiled. "Gestures," she said. "See? You can do them if you want to. Look, I'll sneak you out some goat's cheese with chives. Your favourite. Nobody will know."

I shook my head. "Can't risk it," I said. "Anyway, it's no big deal. I've been eating Beloisa porridge since I was fifteen, and sleeping in ditches."

She sighed. "Spoiled rotten, that's what you are. All you rich kids are the same."

⌣

I THOUGHT ABOUT what she'd said as we rode on to Auzon, and it didn't take me long to realise she was right, as usual. I went back through all the marriages in the various Imperial families for the last few generations, as far back as I could remember, which isn't very far, and there haven't been many of them, because of all the civil wars and usurpations and such. Fact; in the last two hundred years there have been thirty-six emperors, of whom nine died in their beds (and three of them were probably poisoned). Of the

65

thirty-six, only ten were born in the purple and only six of them lived long enough to marry. Of those six, five married commoners; the rationale being that whereas the petty kings of lesser nations have to choose their queens for politics and diplomacy, the Emperor of the Robur is so incredibly far above any other mortal that nobody could possibly be his equal, and no other nation could conceivably aspire to a marriage alliance; so, logically, the emperor is free (almost uniquely among humanity) to marry for love. It's the only argument in favour of having the rotten job I've ever come across, and presumably that's why emperors and crown princes are so often the heroes of soppy romances. Anyway, the same principle applies to sons, nephews and first cousins of the Dragon Signet—put it another way, if tradition was to be observed and the prestige of the purple maintained, I really had no choice but to marry out of the gutter. My duty, in fact. Oh well. Guess I have no alternative but to comply. I still wasn't looking forward to telling my aunt, though. She's a bit like that. If you brought her the severed head of the Great King of the Sashan, she'd moan at you for dripping blood on the carpet.

⚊

It's probably the soldier in me; once I've identified an objective, I want to crack on and achieve it—get there first with the most, Sechimer's lightning strike across the frozen river at Three Bridges, all the great cavalry commanders you've ever read about. So I'd made up my mind that we'd get married at Auzon, with the abbot officiating and presumably my Cassite archers as bridesmaids. It didn't quite work out like that. When we got to Auzon, Auzon wasn't there.

Rather a melodramatic way to record a horribly sober fact. By way of background, if by some chance you aren't reading this with the map on the desk beside you, the monastery at Auzon is—was— barely half a mile from the sea. The monks, at one time great traders and seafarers, built a harbour in a superb natural location; necessary, because that stretch of the coast is murder, with sudden squalls, hidden rocks and that ghastly white wall of mist that comes down out of nowhere and cuts visibility to the point where you can't see your hand at arm's length, half an hour after a clear blue sky. Of course, you'd have to be mad to use that mist deliberately, to mask your arrival from the watch towers on Carason Point and Alsingey. But that, it turned out, was precisely what they'd done, or so the handful of survivors from the village told us. Apparently there's these tiny skerries about ten miles out, where ships piloted by suicidal lunatics could lie up until the fog rolled in. Mist means no wind, so they must have rowed across, ten miles completely blind and somehow avoiding the Devil's Teeth and that vicious rip-tide. Then say five hours to reduce the monastery to rubble and ash, and back out to sea again before the fog thinned.

Speaking as a military man, I despise fighting against lunatics. I've done it once or twice, and it sets your teeth on edge. You can't predict what they'll do, you don't share the same frame of reference regarding the definitions of victory, defeat, surrender or acceptable losses; if they lose, you find yourself staring at a battlefield piled obscenely high with their smashed, slashed bodies, and if they win, they'll probably burn you alive in a wicker cage. Really, they shouldn't be allowed to make war. It's bad enough as it is without all that sort of thing.

This time, as well as slaughtering the monks they'd butchered nearly all the villagers as well, and burnt the farms and barns. Call me a sissy, but I don't hold with all that. Also, it made dreadful problems for us, since we'd been relying on the monastery and the village for provisions for the Cassites and, most of all, fodder for the horses. The best we could do was hobble them and turn them off to graze on what they could pick out from the heather and the gorse. That's no way to treat good livestock if you want them to give of their best.

"Aren't you going to bury them?" she asked me.

"No point," I said. "Burnt bones aren't a health risk, and the rain'll wash the ashes away in a day or so. It's unburnt bodies that cause the plague."

"Yes, but—" She shrugged. "You can't leave people's skulls and bones just lying around. It's not decent."

"No," I said, "it's horrible. But if we stay here and collect them all up and dig a big hole, we won't have enough food to get back to Sambic, let alone press on to Cort Varon. It'll have to go on the big list of things to be done later by someone else."

She frowned. "Do you have to make a lot of decisions like that? I suppose you must do."

"All the time," I said. "And each one is truly bad. All that can be said for them is that the alternatives are even worse."

But she'd made me think, and I compromised. I sent the Cassites back to Sambic, under the command of my senior tribune, and I made her go with them. The other eight tribunes, the six lancers of her escort and I stayed there until we'd picked up all the skulls—the hell with arms and legs—dug a big hole and buried them. By then it had started to rain. I recited something or other from the Long Catechism, and then we wriggled into our oil-skins and made a dash for it. I had ash on my hands all the way back to Sambic. It ran in the rain and turned into little black muddy rivers, all down my trousers.

DECISIONS; AH, DECISIONS. I signed my first death warrant the day before my sixteenth birthday. The poor bastard I condemned was guilty of cowardice in the face of the enemy. Imagine it. You know what a Sashan phalanx looks like, a thousand men wide and fifty deep, but all you see as they come towards you is those terrible long spears, like a forest sideways—a forest that was planted by some optimist who lost interest and never got around to thinning the saplings, so the trees are far too close together, so they shoot straight up to get to the light. Actually, it's not the sight that gets to you, it's the sound, fifty thousand hobnailed boots hitting the deck at *exactly* the same moment, and the ground really does shake, it goes in through the soles of your feet like a tapeworm and strangles your heart. For two seconds you can't think of anything at all; the third second, all you can think about is how you're going to run away with all these people blocking your path. I signed the warrant six hours after the captain of my personal guard grabbed hold of my horse's bridle to stop me hauling right round and bolting like a rabbit. I felt so utterly ashamed, for nearly running and for killing a man who did what I tried to do. My tears splodged the ink. They had to copy it out again, and I had to sign it again. Then I was sick, all over the tribune's shiny boots.

It gets easier with time, but not because you develop into a better person.

On the successful completion of my first campaign, uncle had me made a Companion and awarded me the headless spear, which is the highest honour a soldier can receive. Looking back on it, eighteen years later, I recognise that, yes, I fought a damn good war. I broke a Sashan phalanx with intelligent use of terrain, light infantry and field artillery. I followed up well but resisted the temptation to pursue too closely, which so often leads to last-minute disaster. I had two old steelnecks to advise me, but the overall strategy and the detailed battlefield tactics were my own (well, taken from the *Art of War,* volume six, chapter three; but their man must've read the same books). We stopped an invasion of the Eastern mountains dead in its tracks, and as a result were able to negotiate a peace that lasted for five years, which was the record until quite recently. I was sixteen, for crying out loud, and what I remember most vividly was pissing my trousers. My uncle was thirty-three—my age now—before he got his first command, and he lost three battles and eight thousand men. I think I coped all right. I shouldn't have had to.

I know that I beat the Sashan because their general was an idiot. They had an idiot for a general because they execute all the good ones, in case they try and seize the throne. My uncle was a good general. He seized the throne, burned down half the City and slaughtered his predecessor's family like sheep. What can you do?

※

STACHEL WAS APPALLED when I told him what had happened. The library, he kept saying, my God, the library. When eventually he pulled himself together, I got him to give me his very best maps of the North coast, the old ones that bothered to show all the islands. Also, I said, I needed him to perform a wedding.

He stared at me. "You must be out of your tiny mind," he said.

"It's an emotion often compared to madness, but only in poetry. Come on, you're a priest. It's what priests do."

"Not on your life," he said, and he actually backed away a couple of steps. "You they'll exile. They'll kill me. That's what happens to witnesses."

"It'll be fine," I told him. "I'm just following precedent. Politically—"

"I've already been in one condemned cell," he said. "Two in one lifetime is too many. Look, we were friends once. Don't spoil it."

I balled my fist so he could see the signet ring. Actually it was the fake, which I wear because I'm scared I'll lose the real one. "I'm giving you a direct order," I said.

"Go fuck yourself," said my friend.

※

WELL; A PRIEST is a priest is a priest, and even the most weasel-faced administrator from the Clerk of the Works' office is pervaded by and marinaded in the Holy Spirit, provided he's passed the relevant exams. After six refusals I found an ordained minister who was prepared to marry us, in return for a cash sum and a sinecure on the Eastern frontier. The job took six minutes, and as soon as we were done, the Holy Father jumped on a cavalry horse, slung clinking saddlebags over the pommel of his saddle and thundered out of the main gate in a cloud of dust. If he yelled a blessing over his shoulder as he left, it was drowned by the thunder of hooves on the planks of the drawbridge.

For medical reasons we postponed the traditional wedding-night activities; instead, I sat up into the small hours reading reports that had just reached me from Cort Acuila, where the six-hundred-year-old monastery had been burnt to ashes by raiders who rode down out of the morning mist on small, stocky ponies.

⌣̈

"FORTUITOUSLY," COUNT TRABEA said, "we had a routine patrol out that way. They picked them up the day before and followed them in, so they were able to see what happened."

The Count had rushed to my side, which was nice of him. He'd brought five hundred local militia; also, rather more usefully, two dozen very competent clerks and a big folder of maps. "Fine," I said. "It didn't occur to your men to intervene?"

"There were twelve of them," he said. Well, fair enough.

After the massacre, the raiders had loaded their plunder onto pack-horses. I questioned the patrol myself; what did the raiders take? They were very sorry, but they didn't dare get close enough to see. Whatever it was, the raiders put it in sacks, which they appeared to have brought with them. Heavy sacks or big bulky ones? Just sacks, the patrol leader said. We were six hundred yards away. All right, how many sacks on each horse? Two on some, four on others. Anyway, after that they trailed the raiders across the moor. They made straight for the coast, to a little cove much used by the local smuggling community, where five ships were waiting for them. They turned the ponies loose before they sailed away, and the patrol caught some of them and looked for brands, but there weren't any. So they brought a few back with them, and one of the locals, a bit of a trader when he wasn't mending pots and pans, reckoned he'd seen ponies like them in the Fleyja Islands, which he'd visited once when he was a boy. Nobody else had ever seen anything like them. The local horseflesh is squat and stocky but taller at the shoulder and with a much bigger head.

"So these pirates come from the Fleyja islands," I said. "Does that sound likely to you?"

Trabea thought before answering. "I'd be very surprised," he said. "Of course, I've never been there, and I don't know a lot about them, nobody does. But the impression I've formed over the years is that they're just a bunch of small-time crofters, dead keen to trade with us, because we seem to want all manner of garbage they've got no use for, like beaver-skins and amber, and picking up trash off the beach and trapping vermin is a much easier way of getting food than growing it yourself."

"Stealing's even easier," I said.

He shrugged. "Maybe. And maybe we come across as soft, leaving all those valuable things lying around with just men in dresses to guard them. But they're not stealing food, they're stealing gold and silver and works of art. As far as we know, the only people they trade with is us."

I remembered something I'd seen; affluent City merchants roughing it at the *Hope of Redemption*. Now one of the defining characteristics of the Empire is that it's very big; also, it contains a good number of rich, cultured men who value fine art and beautiful objects rather more than conventional morality. Would a wealthy banker in, say, Procopia worry too much about the provenance of a magnificent Mannerist icon, if he was offered it at the right price? And who would ever recognise a specific piece from the other side of the world, with enough certainty to identify it as stolen property? And plain gold and silver can be melted down into bullion, which tells no tales.

"I've got some orders for you," I said.

"Gosh," Count Trabea said politely. "Just bear with me while I get something to write on."

An immediate embargo on ships from the Fleyja Islands. Spot checks on the goods of merchants. A full investigation to ascertain whether items stolen from the monasteries were turning up on the market anywhere inside the Empire. "And when you've done that—"

"Hold on a minute," Trabea said. "No disrespect, but how many officers do you think I've got? For a start, I'm going to need ships. I've got three customs sloops and a ceremonial barge."

I wrote him a chit. "Twelve warships," I said. "That'll have to do."

He stared at me. "I think we ought to be able to manage with that," he said quietly. "How about soldiers?"

Not quite so easy. The twelve galleys weren't a problem, since I happened to have twelve galleys at my disposal at that particular moment. They'd been assigned to me for sabre-rattling purposes in my negotiations with the Sashan, and I'd sort of neglected to give them back. Soldiers are different. For entirely sound historical reasons, individual commanders don't get to keep soldiers once they've finished with them. If I wanted more than fifty men, I'd have to write to my aunt and say Please nicely. "I'll see what I can do," I said. "Meanwhile, though, I suggest you improvise. You've got a hell of a lot of non-military manpower—road-menders, clerks, grooms, all those men on your payroll that feature so prominently in your accounts. Give them a spear and a shield each and tell them to look warlike. They're not going to have to fight anyone, so who'll know the difference?"

✖

I WROTE TO my aunt; to my great surprise, she promised me a thousand regular steelnecks, due back from the Mesoge any day now. I was stunned. Steelnecks are gold dust, and not entrusted to just anyone; they have a nasty habit of choosing who'll be the next emperor, even when there isn't an immediate vacancy. At least that answered one question I hadn't dared ask. She couldn't have heard about my wedding. If she'd done so, steelnecks would have been sent, but not for me to command. As it was, as and when one of those fast chaises showed up to take me home, a thousand regular heavy infantry would give me the option of not going, if I really didn't want to.

Interesting times.

✖

SHE INSISTED ON coming with me to Cort Maerus. I told her I was deeply touched but it was a tough journey and she really wasn't well enough yet. Patiently she explained that it'd be much easier to murder her if I wasn't there, should anyone wish to do so. I had one of those moments where your guts turn to water, and said yes, of course she was coming. In fact, I wasn't going to let her out of my sight.

Cort Maerus is a long way north. Snow lies on the mountains all year round, though you can grow grapes and figs in the valley; the monks used to have extensive orchards and vineyards a hundred years ago. Now they're just nettles and briar entanglements, and nobody seems to know why. Sheep graze where barley once grew, and every half-mile or so you come across ruined cottages and farmsteads, and nobody could even be bothered to steal the stone. I read everything I could find (there isn't very much) and asked everyone who might know, but there's no memory of any raiders or invasion, no plague, no specific disaster. Once there were a lot of people in those parts, making a good living, and now there are very few, quietly starving. My own theory, for which I have no real evidence, is that their well-earned prosperity was their downfall. Sturdy, well-fed peasants are proverbially the best recruits for the heavy infantry, and we've had ever so many wars in the last two hundred years. I think all those strong, self-reliant farmers' sons went off to war and didn't come back, and without them the place just died. If so, does it say something about the nature of the beast called

Empire? The idea is that Empire protects the towns and villages and little farms from the enemy, and in order to do so recruits soldiers, so that the towns and villages and little farms won't be laid waste, and grass won't grow in abandoned streets and good productive land won't be smothered in weeds and briars. But if the act of protection brings about the destruction it was designed to prevent—well. I'm not a trained philosopher, so I'm not qualified to comment.

Unlike most of its sister houses, Cort Maerus isn't built on a hilltop. It squats comfortably in a valley, where the rainwater comes tumbling down the mountains in a broad river and splays out in a dozen useful little rivers across the flat valley floor. My abiding memory of it is a hundred subtly different shades of green; from the pale green of new shoots of bracken, which grows so well where there's been extensive burning, to the dark, waxy green of well-established ash and willow, quick and efficient colonists of abandoned pasture. There was a narrow road between head-high tangles of briar and dead brushwood, out of which spindly trees shot up gasping for daylight. One of my tribunes, a keen sportsman, had brought along his beautiful new Aelian bow, hoping to pot a few deer, or at the very least the odd rabbit. He never got the chance. We saw any amount of little twittery birds but nothing living at ground level. No animal bigger than a mouse could live in that horrible tangled mess.

The abbot of Cort Maerus was a big, jolly man, who was overjoyed to see us, because he rarely set eyes on anyone he hadn't known for twenty years. He wasn't quite so cheerful when we explained that we hadn't brought much food with us, imagining that he'd be able to feed us; six hundred archers, seventy general staff, my wife and me. He recovered well from the shock. One of the principal duties of the monasteries, he said, was to provide hospitality for hungry travellers, and if that meant that he and his monks would have to tighten their belts a bit that winter, the pleasure of our company would be more than sufficient recompense. In any case, they had plenty of dried beans, and the villagers could be prevailed upon to spare oats for our horses, and a little bacon goes a long way in a nourishing soup. Also, if we hadn't tried the local speciality—nettle soup with tiny bits of diced sausage—we had a real treat in store.

There were forty monks at Maerus, all over fifty. Mostly they worked in the ten-acre walled garden, of which the abbot was enormously proud—fresh cabbage all year round, and heavy crops of roots, which store so well for the hungry months. He showed me a great long gallery above the main dormitory, crammed to the rafters with shelf upon shelf of dull, waxy-skinned apples; he thought it was once the scriptorium, where they used to copy out books, but he couldn't be sure. The old library had been gutted and was now a splendidly dry wood store; a place this size took a lot of heating and it could be bitter in winter, but his people were hard workers and skilled foresters; they coppiced the willow-brakes and the overgrown hazel, and made trips up the mountain with a big old cart to fell the huge pines and firs that grew on the side-of-a-house slopes. Good honest work, he told me, is the closest way of achieving communion with the Creator of All Things, the universal gardener who grew us all from seed. He had short, dirty fingernails and forearms like a blacksmith, and it made me feel tired just listening to him.

"I heard about that," he said, when I mentioned the raiders. He made it sound like interesting gossip from a faraway country of which we know little. "But I can't imagine they'll want to come here. We don't have any gold or silver, we sold all that stuff years ago."

We were sitting in the main chamber of the abbot's lodgings. It was bitter cold, so we sat practically nose to nose on either side of a small brass brazier. It had been there a long time, because its smoke had blackened a wide patch of the ceiling, blotting out the Invincible Sun *orans*, flanked by grubby cherubim with tar-smudged halos. It was too dark to see the rest of the mosaic—I'm woefully ignorant about art, but my guess is, it's early Figurative, probably complete under all the soot and congealed fat from the tallow candles, because the damp didn't seem to have penetrated that far. "Anyway," he said, "if they come, we'll be ready. We've got a plan worked out. There are shepherds' huts up on the mountain, we can gather our tools and supplies for a month at the drop of a hat, and nobody can get into this valley without us seeing them. As you probably noticed, there's only one path through the furze."

I stooped, and shot out a hand instinctively to stop him. "What are you doing?"

He looked at me blankly, then understood. He'd lifted the lid of a big wooden chest and taken out a book. He'd been about to put it on the brazier. "Would you like it?" he asked.

I couldn't read the lettering on the spine, it was too faded. "Thank you," I said, and took it from him. He opened the box, took out another one and threw it on the stove. I didn't try and stop him.

"Nobody reads them any more," he explained. "And books aren't the way to salvation, we realised that a long time ago. Waste not, want not, that's our philosophy here."

The book had thick wooden covers, which burned long after the paper had flared away. It produced a surprising amount of heat. You've got to be practical, the abbot told me gravely. The book I'd rescued turned out to be Frontinus' commentary on Annius, of which there are tens of thousands of copies in every major city in the empire. I've never read it; not my sort of thing.

We didn't stay long at Maerus. They were very pleasant to us, but we didn't want to be a burden. On, instead, to Cort Neva, three days' trudge inland, though mostly downhill, thank God.

I was very glad I'd brought my wife with me, because otherwise the abbess of Neva would have been a problem. I recognised her straight away; hard not to. Seven years earlier, she'd caused havoc at Court. Rumour has it my aunt tried to have her poisoned; if that's true and she failed, it's a striking tribute to Abbess Honoria's intelligence and resourcefulness, because when my aunt wants something done, it generally happens. I could see why my aunt would have wanted rid of her. Intelligent, beautiful aristocratic young widows with money and ambition are about as welcome at Court as locusts in a vineyard. She's a distant cousin, apparently. I wouldn't have been her food-taster for all the gold in Blemya.

Seven years in the frosty north had tightened the skin of her face, and the backs of her hands were a dead giveaway, but she'd still have been a force to be reckoned with if I hadn't had the woman I loved by my side more or less constantly. *Tell me everything that's been happening at Court,* were practically her first words to me, and I don't think she meant hemlines or whether hair was off the shoulder this season, though that was what I told her about. She pretended to be frightfully interested, and I promised to send her a couple of bolts of Priene silk, as soon as there was room on a courier's coach.

"We're terribly worried about these raids," she said, inviting the big, strong man to take care of her. In fact, she'd taken the precaution of hiring seventy Vesani mercenaries, practically as good as steelnecks and much cheaper to maintain. She could afford to, since she'd just sold a Ctesippus altarpiece for two million hyperpyra, to an anonymous buyer from the East. Seventy good men could hold those walls against a thousand regulars. She'd quartered them in the stables, which she'd had made over into a big, comfortable barracks. She still had two Ctesippus icons and a Frontinus triptych of the Ascension, for which she was considering a number of serious offers. As good as a cellarful of arrows and catapult bolts, she told me with a grin, and I agreed with her. You couldn't sell a Ctesippus without a provenance, even in the remote East. But a legitimate one would man your walls and fill your armoury for ten years. She always was smart, that one.

If she was mildly surprised when I asked to see the library, she recovered well, though she summoned the librarian to give the actual commentary. The library building was spotlessly clean, no dust on any of the surfaces and the slate floor gleaming. It had all the standard works in uniform modern bindings, every book numbered and in its proper place at all times, the chains drooping like ripe beans off the vine. There was no-one else in there when we went round., I suspect casual readers weren't encouraged. They'd have made the place look untidy. Sister Librarian was obviously very proud of her charges. I saw pots of lanolin, for greasing the spines so they wouldn't dry out and crack. That would make the book sticky and awkward to hold, but I got the impression that wasn't much of a problem.

"It's a tremendous privilege to be here, of course," abbess Honoria told me, for the fifth time, "and I'm enormously proud to head up such an important institution. I don't miss the old days at all, and it's wonderful to be doing His work in this sublimely peaceful place." On the other hand, she didn't say, and didn't have to. I've only ever seen that sort of hunger in the eyes of neglected dogs; *rescue me, please, before I wither away and die.* A wicked thought crossed my mind; if I wrote my aunt and told her I'd married Honoria, she'd be so relieved when she found out the truth that she'd strew our marriage bed with flowers. But I could be wrong, and the food in the North tastes so strong, you wouldn't notice an out-of-the-ordinary flavour until it was too late, and I was a married man now, with responsibilities.

⚯

Cort Bealfoir was my idea of how a monastery should be. The buildings were small and very old, with a high wall and a strong gatehouse. Inside there was one long dormitory with a refectory over it and a functional reredorter out back; the rest of the site consisted of a magnificent Archaic chapel, a beautifully decorated chapter-house and a huge library/scriptorium, with floor-to-ceiling glazed east-facing windows. Sixty brothers worked there, nearly all of them copying books, under the less-than-rigorous command of Abbot Gennasius, author of the famous *Twelve Questions*.

I'd read his book when I was fourteen and had no idea he was still alive. I wanted to ask him about it, but he fended me off politely with answers polished smooth from decades of use, and we talked about the raids instead. Faced with the terrifying unknown, he'd fought back with the full armoury of scholarship; he'd collated every reference in the Early Fathers to swarms of unidentified savages, and was able to prove to me conclusively that this lot weren't any of them. He'd had copies made of every *Art of War* and *Soldier's Mirror* in the catalogue, ready to be sent to anyone who needed them; I was presented with bound copies, and was too embarrassed to mention that I'd got them all already. He also had chapter and verse ready to justify the use of deadly weapons by contemplative monks in defence of their books and lives. He didn't have any deadly weapons to go with them and I promised him fifty longbows and twenty suits of armour of an obsolete pattern, which I'd noticed in Trabea's inventory. He was as pleased as a cat with two tails, and promised to drill his monks as rigorously as a steelneck sergeant. I'd have loved to have seen that, but I never got the chance. I imagine he'd have used the *Institutions* of Florian rather than the *Manual of Military Practice*, which is later and prone to textual corruption, due to an uncertain manuscript tradition.

From Bealfoir to Cort Erys, down the horrible North Road, which needs a lot of money spending on it before it could count as a goat-track, let alone an artery of empire. Talking of goats; plenty of wild ones in the combes and valleys, and the Cassites were good shots, so we had plenty to eat, if you like goat, which I can't say I do. So we took our time—four days to Erys, and I blame myself. If we'd taken just a few hours longer, I hate to think what the result would have been.

The noise was the first sign of trouble. It was a perfectly still day, and sound travels in the mountains when there's no wind. At first we thought it was a foundry or an arms factory, except there aren't any in the North any more, but monks can be very enterprising, maybe they'd built a steel mill or a mine. It was definitely a clashing, thumping noise, and when we got closer we could hear yelling as well. At that point we knew exactly what we were listening to; once heard, never forgotten, believe me.

It's one of the weird things about this world and human life generally. Two miles from a full-scale battle, where men are being hacked to pieces with sharp tools, you'll see sheep grazing and rooks lining up on the branches of trees overhanging the ripening corn, as if they were the subject of the picture and the confused human events nearby are merely a minor detail in a corner of the background. I've never run away from a battle in my life—too scared to, if the truth were known—but suppose you did, and when you stopped to catch your breath, all around you there's ordinary everyday life, the sun shining, the river flowing. You'd have to stop and ask yourself, which is real, this or the hideous unnatural mess going on where I just came from? It has to be one or the other, it can't be both; because if the two can co-exist, separated only by a little bit of geography, why would anyone in his right mind be down there when he could be up here?

⟓

I HAVE MANY sterling qualities. Moving silently and avoiding observation aren't two of them. I sent scouts, who reported that a large body of men, at last fifteen hundred, were attacking the monastery with ladders and a battering-ram. I got that helpless feeling that always hits me when I know I've got to fight. I'm not sure how to describe it, because there's nothing else like it. I'm terrified, I know it's all going to end very badly, but I have no doubt in my mind whatsoever about what I'm going to do. It's like I'm looking down a tube or a tunnel at the future, a point in time when I've done it all and I'm watching the result, almost like I'm suddenly living my life backwards. I know that I've got to lead with a weakened centre to draw them in, while looping round the left flank to take them by surprise when they burst through, because I've already seen it happen. It doesn't always work, of course. Sometimes it goes spectacularly wrong, and then I'm back to making it up as I go along, a skill at which I do not excel.

The situation in a nutshell. Cort Erys; a modest foundation, on top of a steep hill, a wall all round it, with one gate, protected by a three-storey gatehouse. The bad people—ant-sized, but occasionally flashing in the sun, suggesting at least some armour—seemed to have given up on the ladders and were concentrating their efforts on the gate. The regular thumping noise we'd heard a mile away was the ram. The monks were doing something to annoy them; twinkles in the air told me the raiders were shooting arrows at them to keep their heads down, but clearly with indifferent success. The scouts' estimate of fifteen hundred struck me as being on the conservative side. I had six hundred archers, and to reach the enemy I'd have to descend a steep slope and cross four hundred yards of open ground. The Cassite bow is a marvellous thing, capable of shooting two hundred yards at maximum elevation, but how many shots would they get before the enemy reached us and swept us away? That was assuming the Cassites hung around long enough to be reached, a big and unwarranted assumption. Conclusion; this was a fight I couldn't expect to win.

A wise man once said; the best way to fight is not to fight. It sounds really profound (most statements that scrape the paint of nonsense tend to, I find) but there's a germ of wisdom in it. My job was to find a way of not fighting that would achieve the objective. Luckily, practically everything has been done before at some stage, and I've read an awful lot of books.

Only a lunatic would divide a small army into two and attack the enemy at the extreme edges of his formation, particularly with inferior numbers. To do so would be to invite his opponent to envelop his two wings and wipe them out to the last man. The Emperor doesn't give command of his armies to lunatics; they must know that, even in the Fleyja Islands, or wherever these people were from. Thus it would be logical to assume that the two detachment of lightly-armed archers advancing on the raiders were simply an advance guard, skirmishers; and the apparent tactical error was part of some typically fiendish Imperial stratagem, which would inevitably lead to the total annihilation of the enemy.

The raiders weren't born yesterday. Long before the first archers were in range, they dumped their ram and drew back, in no particular order; when the archers kept on coming, they turned on their heels and ran. That was exactly what happened at Sanga Cuona, and isn't it nice when history repeats itself?

Well, almost. My fault, I guess, for not having paid more attention to the map. If I had, I'd have known that the vector of their probable flight was directly into a dense wood, just over the skyline. Now put yourself in the raiders' position. An Imperial army takes you by surprise. Wisely you withdraw, only to find you're being shepherded into that classic killing ground, the dark forest, in which you can bet your life the crackerjack Imperial general has previously stationed a huge detachment of his dreaded heavy infantry. What can you do? You shy away like a startled animal, double back on your tracks and run like hell for the rapidly narrowing gap between you and the advancing Imperials. If you're lucky, you might just make it; and if you almost get there in time but not quite, desperation leaves you no alternative but to try and punch your way through.

I remember yelling "Get out of the way!", just before one of the bastards ran into me and knocked me spinning. I don't know if he hit me with his shield or I was simply in its way; the iron rim smacked into my eye-socket and I felt the rivets drag across my eyeball.

I had, and still have, a very fine helmet, with a broad steel brim. I wasn't wearing it, of course. Commanders don't, when they're leading from the front. The men have to be able to see it's you, out there being recklessly brave.

I was still on my feet when some other bastard stabbed me, in passing, like an afterthought. The swordpoint skidded off my expensive breastplate and down into my thigh. I was still on my feet. Someone else cannoned into me and sent me down. With my working eye I saw a boot, complete with hobnails—one was missing; top left, from memory—bearing down and blotting out the light. Turning my head away was sheer instinct. The boot and its owner's weight landed on my ear, and for a moment I thought my head was going to burst. Then I was out of things for a bit.

What happened next, so I'm told, is that the tribune Bagoas (who never liked me much) threw himself in front of me and took the spear that should've finished me off. He fell across me—it was his blood, not mine, that I woke up soaked to the skin with, though I didn't know that at the time—and immediately the standard-bearer Leuxis took his place; he cut down four of five of the bastards before they did for him, and by then Teutomer and Gontharius, two of the coach-escort steelnecks, had hacked their way across and stood over me chopping and stabbing like maniacs until the danger was past. They got badly cut up for their pains. Teutomer lost his left hand, and they cut off Gontharius' chin and a slice of his jaw. I can't begin to find words for how I feel about that. I'm sorry, but I can't imagine doing that for anyone, let alone someone I barely know.

⚮

I CAME ROUND in the monastery, with a little old man leaning over me dabbing at my face with a tuft of bog cotton. I knocked his hand away (because the last man I'd seen had been trying to kill me) and he tutted and tried again. I grabbed his wrist. He took the cotton from his trapped hand with his free hand and went on dabbing. The effort was too much for me and I went back to sleep.

When I came round again I was alone. Above me was a gorgeous fresco of the punishment of the damned, and for a moment I wondered if I'd died and was in real trouble. There was something really big and sharp and painful in my left eye, a grain of sand or something like that, and I couldn't see through it because some fool had trussed it up with bandages. My cheekbones ached, right down into my chest. Past experience identified the other pain as a cracked rib. Here we go again.

Then a thought occurred to me, and I started to panic. I tried to get up, but some fool had taped me to the bed with bandages. I tried yelling, but my voice came out as a little froglike croak, so I drummed my feet up and down like a little kid; it sounded very odd, and I realised I was stone deaf in one ear. But it must've worked, because the door opened and she came in, and there was no need to panic any more.

"You're all right," I said (and it sounded very far away). "I was worried."

She knelt down beside me. "I'm fine," she said. "You're not."

Another of those moments. "How bad?"

"They don't know yet," she said. "They may have saved the eye, or they may not."

She was sitting on my left side, which was fortuitous, since I couldn't seem to hear with my right ear, the one that got trodden on. Then; oh.

"The deafness will be permanent, apparently," she said. "Actually, you were very lucky. An inch to the right—"

I couldn't help myself. I burst out laughing.

THEY SORT OF saved the eye, more or less. I can't see much through it, just blurry shapes, and bright light gives me a splitting headache. Actually, I really ought to have died. The crushed ear went bad and the fever set in, and I was a real mess for four days. The little old tutting man pulled me through, apparently; turns out he was the best doctor in the North, with fifty years of experience, all of which he needed to keep me from quietly drifting away. So many people went to so much trouble over me. I can't understand it, but I'm grateful.

As soon as the news reached him, Count Trabea sent his personal physician to look after me. He arrived while I was still out of my head with the fever. My wife and newly-promoted tribune Scaeva intercepted him, told him I was out of danger and sleeping peacefully, and entertained him with fortified wine and honeycakes while Brother Cellarer and Brother Herbalist went through his medicine-chest, opening and sniffing all the bottles and feeding samples of anything they didn't like to a dozen or so caged rats. Disappointingly, the rats came through completely unscathed, and the good brothers couldn't find anything they could possibly take exception to. In due course, Trabea's quack examined me, concurred with everything the little old man had done and told me how lucky I'd been to have such an outstanding doctor when I needed one most. Scaeva was all for planting some poison on him, chopping his head off and having Trabea arrested for conspiracy. I like Scaeva and I'm glad he's done so well for himself, but sometimes he gets a bit carried away.

⁂

AT LAST WE had some dead bodies to look at. They were a bit ripe by the time I was well enough to see them, swollen and purple and no use for anything, but the general consensus was that they weren't the

Fleyja people, who are short and dark, not tall and fair. Captain Eleocarta of the Cassites reckoned they could be Elorians or Cure Doce, while tribune Segimer fancied they might be Aram Chantat from way beyond the Eastern frontier, or possibly no Vei or Rosinholet. Their clothes were crude homespun linen dyed with blueberry juice and their swords and spearheads were the most amazing pattern-welded work, the sort of thing only a handful of smiths in the whole empire know how to do. They caught one live one, but he died of gangrene two days later without saying anything helpful. No amulets, charms or identifiable religious talismans, no rings, earrings or personal items of any kind. Oh, and they were wearing stout, well-made boots. Well, yes, I already knew that.

ERYS, HOWEVER, HAD been saved, so that was all right. And I'm glad about that, because it's a beautiful house; one of the small ones, but with fantastic artwork and a complete set of early Grotesque communion plate, and the best collection of early Robur history and drama anywhere.

The abbot had, he told me, been there practically his whole life; he joined as an eight-year-old novice and turned down four other abbots' mitres and an Eastern see because he couldn't imagine working anywhere else. He was a short, chubby man with a broad face and not many teeth; his speciality, he admitted rather nervously, was the dual procession of the Holy Spirit, which I've never understood and still don't, though he did his best to explain it to me. When not contemplating the awful complexity of the Divine, he ran a cheerful, efficient house that copied more texts per head than anywhere in the North apart from Cort Doce and actually paid its lay brothers for their labours in real money. Anyone in the five surrounding villages could use the mill and the shearing-pens for free, or have their horses shod at the monks' forge at cost, or load their surplus goods on the monks' ship, which made one trip a month down the coast to Aubad. When the raiders came, they'd kept them at bay for two hours by pouring boiling water on their heads—just as well they had ten huge coppers for brewing—and pushing the ladders off the walls with hayforks and winnowing-fans. They braced the gate against the ram with benches from the chapel and beams from the stonemason's crane. Smart people, who didn't lose their heads in a crisis.

"THIS IS NO good," she told me, sitting at my bedside. "First I'm all cut up and then you are."

The same thought had occurred to me. One of the five grounds for annulment is non-consummation.

And beforehand doesn't count; I'd checked. "Sorry," I said. "Put it on the big list of things to do later."

She told me that the scouts had tracked the enemy's retreat back to the coast, where they'd been met by six large ships; they were well out to sea by the time our people got there, so no idea where they were from. Meanwhile, Trabea had taken delivery of his new warships and sent them to cruise off the Fleyja islands; if the raiders showed up there, the fleet would be ready to intercept them.

Stachel came up from Sambic in a rickety old cart, which was all he could lay his hands on at short notice. "God, you're in a state," he said to me. "You want to go easy on that sort of thing. If you're not careful you'll ruin your health."

"Noted," I told him. "Actually, it was supposed to be a bloodless victory. I've always wanted one of those."

"Showing off," he said scornfully. "Serves you right for trying to be clever."

I told him about Trabea's doctor. He seemed surprised. "I still wouldn't trust that creep as far as I could sneeze him," he said. "You must be mad, letting him get his hands on warships." He sat down on the end of my bed, took an apple from his sleeve and bit into it noisily. "Want to know what I think? I wouldn't be a bit surprised if Trabea turned out to be behind all this. Think about it. Everything seems to suggest these pirates or raiders or whatever you want to call them are people we've never encountered before. So you tell me, how do they know where the monasteries are?"

"There's such things as books," I pointed out. "And the monasteries aren't exactly a state secret."

"Yes, but they seem to know their way around the country pretty damn well. Don't tell me they've got detailed maps as well. *We* haven't got detailed maps. You know how I found this place? Followed the map until I was halfway up the wrong mountain, backtracked to the nearest village, had to ask a dozen people before I found one who'd even heard of it. But they know the best way in, the best way out, how to steer through the rocks and shoals, what time of day the fog comes down. Which means," he said, "somebody's telling them."

"Then it can't be one of us," I said. "As you just pointed out, we don't know these things."

He gave me a sour look; don't be flippant. "Trabea's been here a long time," he said. "He's in charge of the taxes and the census. He's got surveyors and mapmakers, plus access to all the best libraries. Also he's got connections in the City to get rid of the stuff. Think about it. The value's in the artwork, not the bullion. If you just melt it all down into ingots, it's not exactly a significant return on the sort of money you'd have to have invested."

Interesting point, but I wasn't immediately convinced. "Not if it's being organised by one of us," I conceded. "But if they're savages from across the sea, who knows how much our stuff's worth where they come from?"

He gave me his patient look. "I think we just established it's not savages," he said, "because of the degree of local knowledge. Which I take to be proven fact," he added. "Look, this isn't like the City, where there's foreigners everywhere you look, or the East. If you were planning something like this out there, sure, you'd send a couple of your people over here to spy out the land, nobody would pay them any mind, they'd assume they were just sightseers. Round here, anybody like that would stick out a mile. Therefore, whoever they are and wherever they come from, it's one of us who's organising it all and, presumably, reaping the rewards. Now ask yourself, who has access to that kind of local knowledge?"

⚮

STACHEL WAS STILL there when the news came in. Cort Maerus, sacked and burned, no survivors, no witnesses; they'd killed the lay brothers and the villagers as well.

"Maerus," she said, "I get confused. Which one was that? Was that the toffee-nosed tart with the bottle hair? If so—"

I shook my head. "Maerus was where they grew all their own food and the roads were clogged with brambles," I said. "I can't make it out. What did they have worth stealing?"

She shrugged. "Maybe they didn't tell you about it. Maybe it was something they didn't know they had."

I pulled a face. "But Trabea did, right? You've been talking to Stachel."

"Actually, Stachel's been talking to me. I think Trabea's far and away your best suspect. I know his sort, believe me."

"Maybe. Or maybe you're both wrong, and it really is just savages, and they don't know what's there until they're inside. This time they were unlucky, you win some, you lose some."

"Oh come on," she said. "Remember what a hard time we had finding the place? It's in a valley, you can't see it from the sea. You'd have to know precisely where to look."

The road ahead of us lay under a natural arch of trees, cut perfectly half-round by the tops of passing wagons. A fine place for an ambush; but the four steelnecks had been through before us and pronounced it safe. We were heading up the long, steep escarpment to Cort Igant, the northernmost of the northern monasteries, a mere twenty miles from the Permian border. The trees were holm-oaks, short and twisted, slow-growing, thriving on steep slopes where carts can't go, no good for planking and miserable to split for firewood, so nobody came to chop them down; you can survive by being contrary and useless. But the road was regularly used, the trees proved that, and someone came along from time to time and filled the ruts and the potholes with gravel from the riverbed, a very long way away, and nobody I'd spoken to seemed to know who. I don't like it when people do essential public works for free, without being asked. It means they're up to something.

Cort Igant practically jumped out at us from among the trees; we turned a corner and there it was, blocking our way like a bandit. The road led straight up to a massive grey gate, which I later learned was three cross-plies of oak. It turned out that there was a back gate and the road carried on out of it, as straight and broad as ever. So; everything that moved along the road went in one gate and out the other. I began to see daylight.

The abbot met us at the gate; he was very friendly, a solemn-looking man just under medium height, with a close-cropped grey beard and neat, short hair. It was an honour to receive such a distinguished guest, and all that sort of thing. He was the first abbot I'd met with inkstains on his fingers, rather out of keeping with the smart, well-groomed rest of him. You can't help getting inky if you do a lot of writing. The foul stuff gets sucked up into the pen and oozes through the thin wall, and next thing you know you're smudging the paper.

"Igant is a relatively recent foundation," he told me, "which means it's only been here four hundred years. In monastic terms, that means the paint's barely dry. But we've been quite fortunate with donors and patrons, and of course we have the revenue from the tolls."

Odd to find an abbot who admits to being well-off. Mostly they plead desperate poverty, so they won't be asked to contribute to one of those strictly voluntary loans my aunt is so fond of. I didn't ask if his people saw to the road-mending. Strictly the business in hand.

"We've heard all about it, of course. Maerus too, such a tragedy. A great house in its day, though I gather it had fallen on hard times. Do you have any idea who these people are?"

No, I didn't say, but maybe you do. "Our best lead at the moment is the Fleyja Islands," I told him. "Only we don't know a great deal about them."

"I think I can help you there," he said quickly. "Our choirmaster was a sailor on a trading ship before he left the world. I believe he went there once."

We walked through the cloister, with a charming garden in the centre. I asked to see the library. The abbot didn't actually express surprise. "Of course," he said, as though I'd just asked him for an elephant. "This way. We have a decent collection, and of course we're adding to it all the time."

And decent enough it was; a smaller building than I'd become used to. The shelves were golden rather than dark brown, and the spines of the books were splendidly uniform, like a regiment of steel-necks on parade; all recent copies, or older books rebound. "Any treasures?" I asked.

"Ah." He smiled. "There is one we're rather proud of."

He showed me a Greater Missal. It was the size of an infantry shield, covered in thin gold sheet studded with gemstones and pearls; possibly the most vulgar thing I've ever seen in my life. "A gift from a generous patron," he said, "who wished to remain anonymous." He turned the pages, and I wanted to shield my bad eye from the glare of the gold leaf. The vellum was milk-white. And that was when the notion that had been struggling up between the paving-slabs of my largely unsatisfactory brain finally burst into flower. "Of course," I said aloud.

"Excuse me?"

"Of course you must respect your donor's wishes," I said. I lifted a couple of links of the chain. It reminded me of the stuff they use for big, savage guard dogs. Perhaps that's what scripture is, though (big, noisy, bites you if you're bad) in which case the precaution is justified.

We toured the defences, which were quite admirable. "I have sixty armed lay-brothers on call at all times," the abbot told me, "we take these things seriously. After all, we're a rich house, and we live in a violent world."

"I don't think you've got very much to worry about," I reassured him.

⚮

"HE'S A SMUGGLER," she said.

I nodded. "Of course he is. And he launders the proceeds by turning them into ghastly works of religious art, and if that's not blasphemy, I don't know what is." I sat down on the bed. I really wanted to rub my bad eye, but I'd been given awful warnings not to. My cracked rib made me whimper. "My guess is that at some stage there'll be a raid and all the gold and silver garbage will be stolen, the abbot and his people will, by some miracle, be away from the house at the time, and they'll retire out East somewhere and divide up the proceeds. Or maybe I'm doing them an injustice and this is their way of glorifying the house of God, I really don't know. In any case, they're a red herring."

I hadn't said what she expected me to say. "Hardly," she said. "Obviously, this is how Trabea gets the stuff out of the empire. Up into Permia, then down the Long River, then overland with the silk caravans to Beloisa and all points east."

"Oh," I said. "Trabea again."

"Of course. And more to the point, that's where the ponies come from, and possibly the men as well."

105

I shook my head. "Permians are dark and brown-eyed."

"Permians are, yes, but there's any God's amount of savages up beyond them we know nothing about, except that they're dirt poor and love to fight. That's where your blue-eyed giants come from, bet you anything you like."

"In any case," I said, "this house has nothing to fear from the raiders, so we don't need to stay here any longer. Pass me that map, would you? I seem to remember there's a river we can follow all the way back to the Doce valley."

"Aren't you going to do anything? He's a smuggler."

I sighed. "Not my problem," I said. "Law enforcement and revenues are Trabea's business. Besides, they've been nice to us, I don't see why we should be nasty to them."

<hr/>

MY UNCLE ONCE said—in public—that I'm too stupid to be allowed out without a keeper. My aunt treats me like an idiot, but she's the same with everyone who's not as smart as she is, into which category falls the rest of the human race and several gods. At the University my tutors said I had a reasonably good mind buried under a coal seam of aristocratic inertia (rather a splendid phrase, don't you think?) but I was always the one who had to have things explained to him by his kind friends after the lecture. In the army, intelligence is like ginger hair; some people have it, some don't, and it really doesn't matter. I have other stirling qualities to compensate. I work hard when there's absolutely no alternative, I bother about details, I try and find the best in people while expecting them to do their worst. And I'm loyal, I will say that for myself.

And I'm lucky. Fool's luck if you like. I get away with things. Fate intervenes to rescue me from the consequences of my ill-judged actions. And I'm lucky with the people around me. For some reason, I seem to attract the most wonderful people, like filings to a magnet—clever, brave, kind, patient, forgiving, resourceful; my wife, of course, and various tribunes and captains who've served with me over the years and won my battles for me and taken spears and arrows that were meant for me. That never ceases to amaze me. Apart from her, I couldn't see myself doing that for anyone.

But I can read, and anyone who reads the right book has an ally, an advisor who's far more clever than he is and can tell him what to do. I have a box of books that goes with me everywhere; my cabinet, terrible pun intended; various *Arts of War* and practical guides to geology, meteorology, agri-culture, economics, sensible stuff; if in doubt, look it up—it's a good, solid box so I can sit on it as well, or stand on it to make speeches, and it stopped a dozen arrows when our camp was attacked at Trigentum. I take the utilitarian view, in other words, probably because I've always been acutely conscious of needing all the help I can get. Accordingly, I'm damned if I'm going to let the accumulated wisdom of the past perish from the face of the earth, whether through damp or fire or being used as arsewipe. And, since I'm not nearly bright enough to know which books are solid gold and which are expendable garbage, I have no alternative but to try and protect them all.

Is that a fault in me? Have I got it wrong? Could I do a lot of harm along the way? A wise man once said that ninety-five parts out of a hundred of all the evil in the world stems from good intentions, and the older I get, the more I believe him. But that could never apply to me, could it, because I *know* my intentions are good—

The first man I killed with a pen died for doing what I'd have done if someone hadn't stopped me. The question is; should I have spared him, or confessed and handed myself in?

⁑

THERE WAS A road to Cort Doce, but we never even got to start. Bright and early in the morning, that sight a general dreads most of all—an Imperial chaise, with outriders.

"She's heard about you," I said. "I'm dead."

"Pull yourself together, for crying out loud," my wife advised me. "Cut their throats, dump the bodies in the woods and say they never got here."

Sound advice, I guess, but I didn't take it. I put on my brave face and went to meet the legate. Turned out I knew him slightly; a sour-faced old boy with a sharp edge to his tongue, staunch ally of my uncle in the House. He handed me a plain brass tube and said, "I'm sorry."

That turned my throat dry. I fumbled with the tube, trying to poke out the rolled-up letter. He took it back and did it for me. I'm useless a lot of the time.

The usual greetings; then—

I have to inform you that your uncle died this morning after a long and painful illness, which he did not bear well.

I have tried to keep this news restricted, but I am well aware that I will not succeed. Our enemies have sources very close to the Signet, and will probably get the news before you do.

For this reason, you cannot return to the City at this time. Proceed to gather whatever forces you can. I have reason to believe that the enemy army is in the north, and it is logical to assume that they will seek to dispose of you, as heir apparent, before marching on the City. Defend yourself as best you can. I regret to say that I have no soldiers to send you on whose loyalty I would be prepared to rely. The commanders of the Sixth, Eighth and Fourteenth Armies are waiting to see what happens; presumably, if you are killed, they will proceed to fight it out among themselves. It is essential for the wellbeing of the Empire that this should not happen, and I therefore urge you to stay alive if at all possible.

Given the resources at your disposal it would be unrealistic to expect you to bring the opposition to battle with any chance of success. I have written to the Great King of the Sashan asking him for troops; at times like these, when our friends are useless or hostile, our best hope lies with our enemy. In theory, the treaty obliges him to send help. In practice, I hope he will prefer the devil he knows, although obviously it will cost us dear in the East. If he refuses, frankly I have no idea which way to turn. It is all most frustrating; if we could field ten thousand men, the problem would be solved, and we pay the wages of a standing army twenty times that size.

Although it is entirely up to you, I strongly urge you to send your wife back to the City with Commissioner Clarus; she will be safe here, at least in the short term, and as the situation deteriorates I am confident I can make arrangements for her to obtain asylum in Scheria or Scona. It goes without saying that I thoroughly disapprove of the match, but at this time it is the least of our problems.

I trust that it is unnecessary for me to tell you how proud I have always been of you, as was your uncle.

If you survive this, I feel sure you will make a fine emperor. I hope very much to see you again.

Your loving aunt,

Eudoxia Honoria Augusta

—and directly under that, the Seal, which I've always thought looks more like a horse than a dragon, but what do I know?

I stared at the letter for a bit. Then I said; "What enemy?"

"The republicans, of course," the legate said. "Didn't you know?"

I WISH PEOPLE would tell me things, instead of assuming I'm omniscient.

The republican movement has always been there, as long as we've had an empire. Get rid of the emperors, give power back to the people—quite; except the people never had any power at any stage in our history, which was probably just as well. In this context, *the people* means the two dozen ancient aristocratic families who own half the land in the empire, the six dozen rich men who hold the mortgages on that land, the priesthood and, of course, the army. They governed the Robur for a thousand years before Florian staged his coup, and because of or in spite of their best efforts we somehow conquered the world. All in self-defence, of course. You'd be amazed how many people we've had to defend ourselves against over the years.

Republicans rebelled against Marianus and nearly won; they gave Detterich a run for his money, and we had to call in the Vesani, which cost us the Delta. It was republicans who assassinated Pacatian and Thrasianus, thereby doing the world an enormous favour, and we're all told to believe that they started the Great Fire. Their heads have decorated arches and gateways for as long as I can remember. I'd never taken them seriously.

"We don't know anything for certain," the legate told me, "but our best intelligence says that they have between four and seven thousand mercenaries standing by on the Permian border—not Permians, probably some new kind of savages we haven't come across yet. Obviously you're their primary target, and then they'll head for the City; at which point it'll be a race to see which general reaches them first and annihilates them. Whoever wins the race will get the City, and then we can look forward to twenty years of civil war, while the Sashan pick off the Eastern provinces."

I shook my head. "They must be mad."

He didn't disagree. "It seems they genuinely believe the City will rise in their favour, and the other cities will follow suit. Quite possibly they're right, except that the army would never let them reach the City." He paused, choosing his words carefully. "The empress believes you're safest if you gather whatever men you can lay your hands on and hole up somewhere, but I'd venture to disagree. If you want my advice, get a ship and head for the Great King's court. The empress is right about one thing, the Sashan are our only hope, and they know you, they know they can do business with you. It's not much of a hope but it's all we've got."

☩

MY WIFE WANTED to stay with me but I nagged her into going back with the legate; mostly because I agreed with my aunt, she'd be safer in Town, but also because if she stayed she'd advise me, and I'd take her advice, because she's probably the smartest person I know. And I knew what that advice would be, and it wasn't what I intended to do.

Trabea could move like lightning when he wanted to. By a sublime stroke of good luck he'd just taken delivery of the thousand steelnecks my aunt had agreed to send him, and they would be the backbone of our army. Add to them my five-hundred-seventy-five remaining Cassites and fifteen hundred local militia, neither useful nor ornamen-tal— And the stupid thing was, I reckoned I knew where I could get a thousand ferocious and highly effective warriors just for the asking, except that I couldn't possibly ask. I did consider it, very seriously. But there are some things I won't be complicit in, even for the empire.

When I told Trabea that I was planning to fight, he went white as a sheet and told me I was mad. But I calmed him down by threatening to cut his head off for embezzlement, and once we'd got that sorted out he proved to be efficient and useful. "It'll be two to one or thereabouts," I told him, pretending to be casual about it, "which is better odds than my uncle had at Boc Gresc, and for all we know, these savages of theirs might turn out to be useless, so—"

He stared at me. "We know they aren't," he said. "Well, don't we?"

I shook my head. "You're assuming the raiders are the mercenaries," I said.

"Well, of course they are. It stands to reason."

"I disagree," I told him, in my subject-closed voice. "Of course they may turn out to be fire-eaters, or they may turn out to be woolly lambs, we just don't know. All we can do is make damn sure we're ready for them."

⚏

TRYING TO TRAIN militia will break your heart, so we didn't bother. Instead, I made a deal with them. Stay where you're put and don't move until you're told to go somewhere else; that's all. Put like that it doesn't sound much, but in fact it's everything—don't run away, even though Death comes charging towards you. I couldn't promise to do it, but they did.

Steelnecks are extraordinary creatures. For them, life is a series of competitions, the Lathrian Games three-sixty-five days a year. They train like lunatics because every month there's a prize for everything—the archery medal, the javelin medal, the laurel wreath for long-distance running in full armour, at company, battalion and regimental level, team and individual. Ten medals automatically gets you promotion, fifteen means double pay, twenty is double pension. On campaign there are endurance awards, and on the actual battlefield there's a long list of prizes and honours, from the Silver Buckle to the Headless Spear. After ten years in the service, gongs and braid are all you're capable of caring about, the honour of the corps and who's where in the league table. What or who you're fighting for, or whether you'll still be alive in the morning, doesn't enter into it. They're even worse than athletes, and without them that guttering flame I talked about earlier would've been snuffed out centuries ago.

Steelneck tribunes are a different kettle of fish altogether. I think I understand a little bit about them, because I used to be one. You take a spoiled rich kid, age about thirteen. You make him live in conditions they'd jib at down the quarries, you send him on twenty-mile marches in full kit and when he gets back, you make him learn Cirra's *Elegiacs* by heart and recite them in front of the whole class; you teach him to be fluent in four living languages and three dead ones, make him learn philosophy like it was weapons drill and weapons drill like it was philosophy; you don't feed him properly, so he's forced to steal food and thereby learn stealth and deception, but if he's caught he's tied to a gate and flogged; when he's sixteen you give him powers of life and death over a hundred steelnecks and send him off to war. Then, if he's one of the few who lives to reach fifty, you enrol him in the House and let him shape the future of the empire. It's a completely ridiculous system, and seems to work quite well.

I've lived with these people most of my adult life, I admire them and some of them I actually like, but I'm not one of them. Not sure I'm one of anybody else, come to that. If I felt at home anywhere it was probably the University—sometimes I wake up and, in that dreamy half-awake-half-asleep interval before you really come to, I'm convinced I'm still a student, with lectures in the morning and the library all afternoon. I was only there for a year, before I had to rejoin my regiment, and to tell you the truth I was always out of my depth, though mostly people were very kind.

SEEK OUT THE enemy and destroy him; quite. I was asking myself how on earth I was going to find the enemy, in a country with seven roads and thousands of forests, combes and valleys, but I needn't have worried. They came to us.

IT TAKES SEVEN years for an apple tree to mature and bear fruit. Roughly seven years earlier, someone—monks, presumably, nobody else would've had the capital—had planted out sixty acres of gently sloping hillside in cider apple trees. Whoever it was knew their business. They'd clear-felled a rectangular tongue into one of those ancient holm-oak forests, so the plantation would be sheltered on three sides and still get plenty of sun; the slope faced west, so it would catch the frost in winter, and frost is essential for setting the fruit. I imagine it must have been monks, and they read about orchard-building in a book; stored wisdom put into useful practice, which is the point of the exercise.

We ruined all that. I drew up my militia half-way down the slope in two long, sparse lines, stretching from the woods on the left to the edge of the steelneck phalanx, five ranks of one-hundred-eighty, hard up against the woods on the right. That left a hundred steelnecks as a reserve and my personal bodyguard. The Cassites—

What I really hated about the plan was the way everything depended on the Cassites. If the enemy believed the message I'd allowed them to intercept, saying that the Cassites had deserted *en bloc*, they'd look to outflank me by going through the woods. If they didn't believe it, they'd assume that I had my archers hidden in the woods, and launch a frontal assault on my paper-thin militia. All I knew for sure about the enemy was that they'd been seen riding in column two days earlier; whether they were cavalry or infantry who preferred not to walk remained to be seen. I had a backup plan, of course, but I didn't like it much.

The mist cleared early that morning, which was a bit of a blow; we'd have the sun in our eyes until noon, and you'd be surprised what a difference that can make on a sunshiny day, which was what that day turned out to be.

Trabea was commanding the steelnecks, so we said our awkward goodbyes quite early. "For what it's worth," I told him, "if by some miracle we win this, I want you to know the slate'll be clean, as far as you and I are concerned. You can keep the money you've been creaming off the poll tax and the harbour dues, and anything else I don't know about, and I'll give you a province out East, where you can really fill your boots."

He laughed. "Thanks, but no thanks," he said. "I've made my pile. That was the idea all along, do ten years in the sticks, then retire somewhere warm and live like a civilised human being. My trouble is, I'm lazy. Fleecing Aelia would be too much like hard work."

I shrugged. "The offer stands," I said. "Good luck. And thanks for standing by me."

"I never really had a choice," he said, and I never saw him again.

Tribune Tarsena made me put my armour on, even though it hurt. "You're mad," he said. "You shouldn't be on the field at all, the state you're in."

"I lead from the front," I told him. "You know that. I wish I didn't have to, but I do." He lifted the helmet off the table. I shook my head.

"You've got to wear it," Tarsena said. "The doctor says—"

"Don't nag, you're worse than my wife."

"The doctor says—"

I backed away, putting the table between him and me. Utterly ludicrous. "If I wear the helmet," I said, "I'll get a splitting headache. If I get a headache, I won't be able to think. If I can't think, we're all going to die. I'll wear the stupid breastplate, and that's it."

"And the greaves."

"Definitely not the greaves. I can't run worth spit with those things on."

He gave me that look. "Honestly," he said, "you're like a little kid."

I scowled at him. "Remember who you're talking to. Like a little kid, *sir.*"

We compromised. I wore the breastplate and the left greave, because you lead with your left leg, and I was excused the helmet. Of course the first thing I did when his back was turned was pull off the greave and hide it under some blankets. Bloody fool I'd look, hobbling around with one greave.

I'd chosen tribune Rabanus to be my chief of staff. That's a fancy way of describing the man who stands next to me so I can have someone to think aloud to; a general who talks to himself doesn't inspire confidence. "Out of interest," I asked him, as the sun caught the enemy spearpoints in the valley below, "what's your real name?"

"Sir?"

"Rabanus isn't a Mesoge name. What do they call you back home?"

He grinned. "I'm Hrafn son of Sighvat son of Thiudrek from Gjaudarsond in Laxeydardal."

"Fine," I said. "I'll call you Rabanus." I peered into the sun. "I can't see a damn thing."

He shaded his eyes with his hand. "They've stopped. They're dismounting."

"Nuts," I said. I'd chosen the field chiefly on the assumption they were cavalry. "What's their order like?"

"Slovenly," said the twenty-year steelneck. "They're just milling about, like a crowd at the races."

"First good news I've heard all day."

That must've puzzled him, but he didn't comment. Good news, because I'd been doing my reading. If, as seemed likely, they were one of the tribes in the far north, it was a reasonable bet that their society was structured round the clan—big chief, his immediate household, then the off-relations and poor relations. In a setup like that, the whole point of war isn't capturing territory or securing lines of communication. You fight to prove how good you are, how many heads you can cut off, with the chief watching; and you can't do that if you're stuck at the back waiting your turn. So they charge; it's a race to see who can get to the killing-ground first, and only the bravest men in the world can withstand a charge like that. Good news? I must've been out of my mind.

I hate the standing-about-waiting stage, but on this occasion it didn't last long. The brown blur in the valley surged forward and started to swarm up the hill toward us. It wasn't long before we could hear them, and I'm ashamed to say the yelling and the howling got to me. I felt that old familiar tugging sensation, the urge to run—I'd have done it if it hadn't been for Rabanus, still as a statue, relaxed, breathing deeply. I started to edge away; he caught hold of my elbow, low down so nobody could see. He didn't say a word. I'd have given a thousand hyperpyra for my helmet and five hundred each for my greaves; better still, a solid iron box with ten padlocks to hide in until it was safe to come out.

"Look," Rabanus said. I was watching the steelnecks. I glanced down the valley, and saw that the brown surge was veering left, to avoid the phalanx and hit the militia. Which was what I'd have done; smash through the weak part of the line, then swing round and take the regulars in flank and rear.

"We're on," I said quietly. "Ah well. Here we go."

The militia had sworn me a solemn oath to stand their ground, no matter what. When the enemy were two hundred yards away, they turned and ran like deer; one moment they were there, the next they weren't, and who can blame them? The only thing that held them up was the trench I'd had dug during the night—sorry, did I forget to mention that?—in which stood my Cassite archers; but it wasn't very wide and most of them were able to jump clean over it, and the rest of them sank to the ground in terror and lay there when the Cassites stood up and started shooting.

It's a cliché to talk about men in a battle falling like grass under the scythe, but I can't think of a better image. The front runners stop in their tracks and drop in a heap; the ones behind stumble over them and pile up as they change from a moving to a stationary target; they fall in windrows, like cut, raked hay, the interval between the rows being the time it takes an archer to take an arrow from his quiver, nock and draw. It's a horrible sight, because those are human beings in those heaps and stacks, living and not-quite-dead buried under the corpses, bleeding to death or buried alive and suffocating. You want the wind to be in the other direction, because it carries away the noise. But it can't last forever. Sooner or later, the men further back figure out what's happening and have the common sense to swerve out of the way. The swarm veers round the tangled mess; the archers adjust their aim and a new windrow forms, but it's a dozen or so yards closer to where they're standing, which means they don't have quite enough time to nock and draw. Most of them realise this; they drop their bows and scramble up out of the ditch, just as the enemy reach them. A few moments later, half of them are dead; the other half are running, and so aren't aware of the solid wall of steelneck shields slamming into the savages' right flank; it's only when they can't run any further and have to stop that they realise there's nobody chasing them, because the phalanx has rolled right over the enemy like a cartwheel over a stray cat.

Steelnecks are pleasant enough people most of the time, but they do like killing, when they get the chance. We shouldn't really encourage them, but we do.

The idea had been that, at the crucial moment when the savages overwhelmed the archers' position, I would charge at the head of my hundred picked men, to give the phalanx time to reform and deploy. In the event, they got there before we did, probably because I'd promised ten tremisses a man and the Bronze Crown to whichever unit contacted the enemy first. It was a cheap incentive, because of the hundred men of D company, only seventeen survived. I don't have any figures fore the enemy dead, because we didn't bother counting. We heaved bodies into the ditch until it was full, and left the rest for the crows.

Trabea was killed, leading D company from the front. Tribune Tarsena was killed when we got in the way of a bunch of terrified savages trying to escape the slaughter; he shoved me aside and let them crash into him, and they trod him into the dirt. Tribune Rabanus was luckier; he only lost two fingers, when he parried a sword-cut aimed at my head with his hand, because his shield had been hacked away. I can't remember if I hurt anyone, on purpose or accidentally; it was all over very quickly, and then those of us who were left just stood there for a while, like we'd just woken up and were wondering what the hell was going on.

We still have no idea who those people were, or where they came from. They were tall, with high cheek-bones and long black hair in braids. They went barefoot, and fastened their cloaks with bronze pins shaped like grasshoppers. That's all I know about them, and I couldn't care less.

꙳

As soon as he saw what had happened, the enemy commander jumped on his horse and rode away. We caught up with him the next evening, in a hayloft. He scrambled out when the soldiers started jabbing the hay with their spears, jumped through the loft door and broke his leg.

They dumped him in a cart and brought him to me. He stank of his own piss. He started to plead. He was pathetic.

"Sorry," I told him. "Not this time." Then I looked past him to the tribune, who nodded, took a long step forward and cut off his head.

So died my good friend Stachel, who used to help me with my Logic essays, and the blood from his neck spurted all over my sleeve, and I had to change my shirt. He died for what he'd always believed in, a better world free from tyranny and oppression, and we buried him in a dunghill. I feel sure he'd have done the same for me.

꙳

I quite like a lot of the old traditions, but not the one where soldiers on the battlefield acclaim the new emperor by raising him on a shield. I was scared stiff I'd fall off and hurt myself and look a fool. Rabanus suggested gluing the soles of my boots to the shield. I think he was joking, but it's hard to tell.

When I reached the City, there were declarations of undying loyalty from thirteen of the fifteen regional commanders-in-chief waiting for me. The other two arrived the next morning, because the courier from the East takes that much longer. I found it really hard to accept. I never wanted to be emperor, and I'd always assumed it'd land on my cousin Scaurus, except that he inexplicably fell out of a high window ten minutes before my uncle died. I'd always thought my aunt liked him much more than me. I don't know, maybe she did. After that, she never once mentioned his name to her dying day, and neither did I.

When I was five yards from the Lion Gate, it opened—not just the wicket, the whole twelve-foot-high embossed bronze monstrosity, and the kettlehats stepped back smartly and presented arms, instead of peering in my face to see if my beard was stuck on with gum.

⌣̈

"It's not so bad," my aunt said, after a careful examination and a long pause. "And you were never a thing of beauty at the best of times."

"That's all right, then," I said.

"Can you see anything at all on that side?"

"Light, colours, vague shapes. Lucky it's not my master eye, or I'd have to learn archery all over again."

She'd actually stood up when I walked into the room. I'd been horrified. She was head to foot in red homespun, which threw me until I remembered that red was the proper colour for mourning where she came from. Sorry, where we came from. A very long way away. "He was a good man, in his way," she said. "He had a chip on his shoulder all his life, about who he was and what he used to be. He was one of those men whose faults make them strong. I won't miss his temper, but I'll say this for him, sooner or later he always listened."

We sat still and quiet for a moment. Then I said, "Why me?"

She didn't smile. "Not for your personal magnetism and giant brain," she said, "that's for sure." She gave me the exasperated look; sit up straight, can't you, don't slouch. "Continuity," she said. "Stability."

"Because I'm family."

She shrugged. "Thousands of unsuitable men inherit valuable property every day for that very reason," she said. "Also, the pool of candidates is restricted; you or one of the generals. If it's one of them, we get a civil war."

"Out of interest," I said, "why haven't we got a civil war? Why have they all rolled over and accepted it? I can't make it out."

She handed me the needle and thread; I licked the end and twisted it into a point so it'd slip through the eye. Long practice. "I think, because none of them want to be emperor badly enough to go through all that again. Your uncle chose them, remember."

"You chose them."

"I gave him the benefit of my opinion. And he chose well. They're none of them military geniuses, God knows, but that's all right, who are we going to have to fight?"

"Let me see. Oh yes, the Sashan."

"Who choose their generals in exactly the same way; not the brightest, not the best, because that only makes trouble." She concentrated on her stitches for a moment. "Will you lead the army yourself?"

"What do you think?"

"Probably you should. You have a knack of being liked by the men, and so long as the army's behind you, you're relatively safe. Besides, it'll give you something to do. Men should have jobs. It keeps them focussed. A man of leisure starts thinking about things, and that leads to trouble."

Ah well, I thought; no peace for the wicked. "But not right away," I said. "I think the treaty will hold for a while yet. I think I'll send a new ambassador. Tellecho's been out there too long, and he's never liked them much."

"What you should do," she said, "except that now you can't, is marry the Great King's sister."

I made an unintended noise. "I don't think so," I said. "She's eleven."

"Your son would have ruled the world. Still," she added, snipping the thread with a tiny pair of gold scissors, "I know it's no use trying to convince you of anything once you're mind's made up."

News to me. "He may yet," I said. "You never know."

She put down the fabric and looked straight at me. "You won't ever have a son," she said, "or a daughter. Not unless you marry again."

I couldn't understand what she was saying for a moment. Then I remembered. *What did the doctor say?* I'd asked her, and she'd hesitated just for a fraction of a second. An inch to the left—

"How many people know?" I asked.

She nodded her approval; it was the right question. "By now," she said, "probably everybody. The generals certainly, and the Great King, and the Vesani senate." She frowned. "She should have told you before she married you."

"It'd have made no difference."

That got me a look. "Well, there you are, then. No point telling the news to a deaf man." Then she put her hand on mine and actually smiled. "I like her," she said, "she reminds me of my friend Svangerd. You know, you met her, the abbess of Cort Doce. How is she, by the way?"

My heart turned to stone. "Actually," I said, "I wanted to talk to you about her."

She was still smiling. "I miss her, you know. Obviously she had to be out of the way while your uncle was alive, but now, I'm thinking of letting her come back. I do so miss having someone my own age to talk to."

Some things you just have to do. "I'm sorry, aunt," I said. "I don't think that's going to be possible."

She stared at me as though I'd hit her. "What did you say?"

I wanted to run away, and there was no tribune to stop me. But; "I'm sorry," I said, "but abbess Svangerd is under arrest. I issued the warrant before I came south."

"What on earth are you talking about?"

Deep breath. There are times when I loathe the sound of my own voice. "Abbess Svangerd is directly responsible for the destruction of the monasteries and the deaths of thousands of people. She's behind the whole thing. She hired the raiders and told them what to do."

"You're mad."

I shook my head. "She wanted the books," I said. "She couldn't bear the thought of all the rare, unique books in the other monasteries being at risk, with people who didn't care about them and weren't looking after them properly. She wanted them all safe at Doce, where she could protect them. I imagine she tried asking nicely first, but when she couldn't get what she wanted that way, she took matters into her own hands. I really am sorry. I know she was your friend."

She was staring at me. "You've got no proof."

"Actually, by now I probably do. I sent a couple of tribunes to Doce with orders to search the place. They know what to look for, the books where only one copy exists, that used to be in the other houses. I've also got the Permian traders who made the contacts with the savages. Quite by chance, we caught a couple of their business partners while we were rounding up Stachel's general staff, and they gave us the names. But that's just the icing on the cake, the books are all the proof we need. And I imagine she'll confess. She didn't strike me as the type who wriggles on the hook." Then a door opened in my mind, and a crack of light gleamed through. "You knew."

She looked at me. "It didn't take a genius to figure it out."

"But you sent me to investigate."

"I wanted you out of the way." Her voice was strained but level. "I knew your uncle didn't have long. If you'd been at Court, they'd have killed you. You were safe in the north."

"It never occurred to you that I'd figure it out."

"No. You're smarter than I gave you credit for." She picked up her sewing, put it down again. "What made you realise it was her?"

"Things she said, and the way she said them. And I knew it had to be the books the raiders were after, because paper leaves a distinctive kind of ash, and there wasn't any like that. And there was nothing worth having at Cort Maerus except books, and they went there anyway. Once I knew it was books, it had to be her or Stachel, nobody else cared enough. And it wasn't Stachel, because he wanted something else. So it had to be her."

I'd never seen her look like that before. She looked old, and frightened. A few days before, she could have had me killed just by nodding.

"Let her go," she said, "for my sake. Please."

My poor friend Stachel, who pleaded with me, his trousers soaked with piss. "I can't do that," I said. "I'm sorry."

☓

THE STEELNECK TRIBUNES found the books in a disused cistern. There was a reference to it in an old book, but the entrance had been cleverly bricked up and disguised, you'd never haver known it was there if you didn't know exactly where to look. But I'd copied it out for them, and they went straight to it. The cistern was a huge space; filled right up with books, so she'd have had to find more storage if she'd carried on. The rarities were in her bedroom, in a cedar linen-press, with a newly-fitted padlock.

I sent her a bottle of poison, but she didn't use it. She told her maids that she knew my aunt would save her. When the time came, they had to drag her to the block and hold her down, a little old lady, my aunt's age. She died pleading, cut off in mid sentence.

I have this habit of killing people for doing what I want to do. One of my first official acts as emperor was to found three Imperial libraries, in the City, at Lonazep and at Beloisa. I appointed a commission of the world's best scholars to catalogue every library in the empire, to find out precisely what we've got, and get copies made so that there's one copy of everything in each of the three. It's been ten years and nobody seems to be in any great hurry, except when I shout and make a fuss. The one in the City will be called the Ultor Library, in honour of my uncle, who didn't learn to read till he was twenty-three and never willingly opened a book in his life.

Among those who pleaded for Svangerd's life was my wife. If I spared Svangerd for her sake, she said, my aunt would love her for it and we'd have no more aggravation out of her. Politically—

I told my wife, who knew she could never have children but didn't tell me, that my aunt would love her just as much for trying.

TEN YEARS; IN eighteen months, it'll be the longest reign in two centuries, and yet it feels like I've barely started. I can't say I've done anything in particular. We beat the Sashan, I suppose; nine battles, of which eight were victories and one was a horrendous defeat, and now the border's more or less where it's always been, and there's a treaty. I still lead from the front, because I've got to, and general Rabanus is always right beside me, to grab my arm and stop me running. I have good people around me and they run the empire as well as it's reasonable to expect.

My aunt has been abbess of Cort Doce for five years now. I don't think she likes it there, but I bet she runs a tight ship. I send her blankets and nice things to eat, but I simply can't find the time to visit.

YOU'RE READING THIS, so it must have survived; been kept, and copied out, and copies made from the copies; it must have a home on a shelf in a library somewhere—possibly one of my three, or maybe they were all burned to the ground years ago; you'll know about that, and I won't, I'm delighted to say. This book has no right to survive on its merits, just as I had no right to survive on mine. We made it this far because my aunt's husband, an illiterate savage called Ultor, won a civil war, in which a lot of innocent people died and a great many beautiful and irreplaceable things were lost. As my aunt said, I represent continuity. All I have done and can do is tend the guttering flame; and if that flame sets the house on fire and burns down the City and the whole world, I guess that'll be my fault too.